CUMBRIA LIBRARIES

WITHDRAWN

KT-545-870

3 8003 03744 4742

1 3 JAN 2011	LH	BAL 11/18
1 MAR 2011		
8 MAR 2011	1 9 MAY 2011	
1 4 MAR 2011	1 8 OCT 2012	17 DEC 2018
- 9 APR 2011	3-1-2013	
2 1 APR 2011	29/6 7-6-16	
2 9 JUN 2011	DHL 1/17	
13/7/11	- 1 FEB 2017	
HAR 1 4 JUN 2012		
28·12·2012		

Cumbria Library Services

County Council

This book is due for return on or before the last date above.
It may be renewed by personal application, post or telephone,
if not in demand.   C.L. 18F

Cumbria County Library
Carlisle Group H.Q.
The Lanes
CARLISLE
CA3 8NX

DOORSTEP
TWINS

DOORSTEP TWINS

BY

REBECCA WINTERS

MILLS & BOON

All the characters in this book have no existence
outside the imagination of the author, and have
no relation whatsoever to anyone bearing the same
name or names. They are not even distantly inspired
by any individual known or unknown to the author,
and all the incidents are pure invention.

All Rights Reserved including the right of
reproduction in whole or in part in any form.
This edition is published by arrangement with
Harlequin Enterprises II BV/S.à.r.l. The text of this
publication or any part thereof may not be reproduced
or transmitted in any form or by any means, electronic
or mechanical, including photocopying, recording,
storage in an information retrieval system, or otherwise,
without the written permission of the publisher.

® and TM are trademarks owned and used by the
trademark owner and/or its licensee. Trademarks
marked with ® are registered with the United Kingdom
Patent Office and/or the Office for Harmonisation in
the Internal Market and in other countries.

First published in Great Britain 2010
Large Print edition 2010
Harlequin Mills & Boon Limited,
Eton House, 18-24 Paradise Road,
Richmond, Surrey TW9 1SR

© Rebecca Winters 2010

ISBN: 978 0 263 21264 8

Harlequin Mills & Boon policy is to use papers that are
natural, renewable and recyclable products and made
from wood grown in sustainable forests. The logging and
manufacturing process conform to the legal environmental
regulations of the country of origin.

Printed and bound in Great Britain
by CPI Antony Rowe, Chippenham, Wiltshire

CHAPTER ONE

"I'm sorry, Ms. Turner, but Kyrie Simonides says he can't fit you in today. If you'll come next Tuesday at three o'clock?"

Gabi's hand tightened around the leather strap of her taupe handbag. "I won't be in Athens then." The outcome of this visit would determine how soon she left Greece…that was if she were allowed to see him now.

She fought not to lose her composure in front of the retirement-age-looking receptionist who was probably paid a lot of money not to lose *hers*. "After waiting over three hours for him, surely he can take another five minutes to talk to me."

The woman with heavy streaks of silver in her hair shook her head. "It's the weekend. He should have left Athens an hour ago."

At twenty after six on a hot Friday evening

Gabi could believe it, but she hadn't come this far to be put off. There was too much at stake. Taking a calming breath, she said, "I didn't want to have to say this to you, but he's left me no choice. Please tell him it's a matter of life and death."

Because it was the truth and her eyes didn't blink, the receptionist's expression underwent a subtle change. "If this is some kind of a joke, I'm afraid it will backfire on you."

"This is no joke," Gabi replied, standing her ground at five feet five in her comfortable two-piece cotton suit of pale lemon. She'd already undergone a thorough vetting and security check upon entering the building, so the receptionist knew she didn't pose a threat.

After a slight hesitation the taller woman, clearly in a dilemma, got up from her desk and walked with a decided limp back to her boss's office. That was progress.

While businessmen came and went from his private domain on top of the building complex in downtown Athens, she'd been continually ig-nored until now. If Gabi had just come out with it in the first place, it might not have taken her most of the day to get results, but she'd wanted to protect him.

Gabi only knew three facts about the thirty-three-year-old Andreas Simonides: First, he was the reputed new force majeure at the internationally renowned Simonides Corporation whose holdings were tied up in all areas of metallurgy, including aluminum, copper and plastics.

Her source confided that their vast fortune, accumulated over many decades, included the ownership of eighty companies. With a population of twelve thousand employees, the Simonides family ruled over a virtual empire extending beyond Greece.

Second, if the picture in the newspaper didn't lie, he was an exceptionally attractive male.

The third fact wasn't public knowledge. In truth no one knew what Gabi knew…not even the man himself. But once they talked, his life would change forever whether he liked it or not.

While she stood there anticipating their first meeting, she heard the woman's footsteps.

"Kyrie Simonides will give you two minutes, no more."

"I'll take them!"

"You go down the hall and through the double doors."

"Thank you very much," she said with heartfelt sincerity, then rushed around the reception desk, her golden jaw-length curls bouncing. At first she didn't see anyone as she entered his elegant inner sanctum.

"Life and death you said?" came a voice of male irony from behind her. Though deep, it had an appealing vibrant quality.

She spun around to discover a tall man shrugging into an expensive-looking gray suit jacket he'd just taken from a closet. The play of ripcord muscle in his arms and shoulders beneath a dazzling white shirt attested to the fact that he didn't spend all his time in the confines of an office. Helpless to do otherwise, her gaze fell lower to the fabric of his trousers molding powerful thighs.

"I'm waiting, Ms. Turner."

Heat stole into her cheeks to be caught staring

like that. She lifted her head, but her voice caught as she looked up into eyes of iron gray, half veiled by long black lashes that gave him an aloof quality.

He possessed a healthy head of medium-cropped black hair and an olive complexion. Rugged of feature, his dark Greek looks fascinated her. The picture she'd seen of him hadn't picked up the slight scar partially hidden in his left eyebrow, or the lines of experience she could detect around his eyes and wide male mouth. They revealed a life that had known every emotion.

"You're a difficult man to reach."

After shutting the closet door, he walked across the room to his private elevator. "I'm on my way out. Since you refused to come back next Tuesday, say what you have to say before I leave." He'd already stepped inside the lift, ready to push the button. No doubt he had a helicopter on the roof waiting to fly him to some exotic vacation spot for the weekend.

Standing next to him, she'd never felt more diminutive. Even if she didn't have an appointment, his condescension was too much. But because she might never have another opportunity to get this close to him, she hid her reaction.

Without wasting time she opened her handbag and pulled out a manila envelope. Since he made no move to take it, she undid the flap and removed the contents.

Beneath a set of DNA results lay the front page of a year-old Greek newspaper revealing him aboard the Simonides yacht, surrounded by a crush of people partying the night away. Gabi's elder half sister Thea, whose dark Grecian beauty stood out from the other women on board, was among the crowd captured in the photo. The headline read, "New CEO at Simonides is cause for celebration."

Along with these items was a photograph taken a few days ago of two baby boys wearing diapers and shirts. Gabi had gone to a store to get it enlarged into an eight-by-ten.

She held everything up so he couldn't miss looking at the identical twins who had a crop of curly black hair and gorgeous olive skin like his and Thea's. He'd had his hair cut since the photo.

Up close she picked out many of the other similarities to him, including their widow's peaks and the winged shape of their dark eyebrows. The strong resemblance didn't stop there. She quickly noticed they had his firm chin and wide mouth. Her list went on and on down to their sturdy bodies and same square-cut fingertips.

Yet nothing about the set of his features indicated the picture had made any kind of impression. "I don't see *you* in the photograph, Ms. Turner. I'm sorry if you're in such a desperate situation, but darkening my doorstep wanting a handout isn't the way to get the help you need."

Gabi's jaw hardened. "And you're not the first man to ignore the children he helped bring into the world."

His black eyes narrowed. "What kind of a mother sends someone else on an errand like this?"

Somehow she got around the boulder in her

throat. "I wish my sister could have come her-self, but she's dead."

The moment the words left her lips, she sensed his body quicken. "That's a tragedy. Now if you'll excuse me."

Andreas Simonides was a cold-blooded man. There was no way to reach him. As his hand moved to the button on the panel, alerting her that this conversation was over, she said, "Are you saying you never saw this woman in your life?"

Gabi pointed to Thea's face in the newspa-per picture. "Maybe this will help." She put the items under her arm while she pulled out Thea's Greek passport. "Here."

To her surprise he took it from her and ex-amined the photo. "Thea Paulos, twenty-four, Athens. Issued five years ago." His black brows formed a bar. He shot her a penetrating glance. "Your sister, you say?"

"My half sister," she amended. "Daddy's first wife was Greek. After she died, he married my American mother. After a while I came along. This was the last passport Thea held before her divorce." Gabi bit her lip. "She…celebrated it with friends aboard your yacht."

He handed the passport back to her. "I'm sorry about your loss, but I can't help you."

She felt a stab of pain. "I'm sorry for the twins," she murmured. "To lose their mother is tragic beyond words. However, when they're old enough to ask where their father is and I have to tell them he's alive somewhere—but it doesn't matter because they never mattered to him—*that* will be the ultimate tragedy."

The elevator door closed, putting a definitive end to all communication. Gabi spun around, angry and heartsick. For two cents she'd leave the incriminating evidence with his receptionist and let the other woman draw her own conclusions.

But creating a scandal within the Simonides empire was the last thing Gabi wanted to do, not when it could rebound on her own family, especially on her father whose diplomat position in the consulate on Crete might be compromised. In his work he met with Greek VIPs in business and governmental positions on a regular basis.

She couldn't bear it if her presence here brought on unwanted repercussions.

No one had asked her to come. Except for Mr. Simonides himself now, no one knew the nature of this visit, especially not her grieving parents. Since Thea had died in childbirth from a heart condition brought on by the pregnancy, Gabi had taken it upon herself to be the babies' advocate. Every child deserved its own wonderful birth mother and father. Unfortunately not every child was so lucky.

"Mission accomplished," she whispered to the empty room. Her heart felt like an anchor that had come loose and had plunged through fathoms of dark water to the lowest depths of the Mediterranean.

Once she'd put everything back in the envelope and stashed it in her handbag, she left his private office. The venerable receptionist nodded to Gabi before she disappeared into the hall. In a few minutes she arrived at the ground floor of the building and hurried outside to get a taxi back to her hotel.

To her surprise, the chauffeur of a limo parked

in front got out and approached her. "Ms. Turner?"

She blinked. "Yes?"

"Kyrie Simonides said you had to wait a long time to get in to see him. I've been asked to drive you wherever it is you wish to go."

Her adrenaline kicked in, causing her pulse to speed up. Did this mean the twins' father wasn't a complete block of ice after all? Who wouldn't melt over seeing a photo of his own flesh and blood? If the boys' picture didn't completely convince him, the printout of their DNA would provide infallible proof of a match.

By sending a limo for Gabi, it could mean he planned for a second meeting with her, but he was forced to be discreet. With his money and power, not to mention his looks, the head man had learned how to keep his former liaisons private.

"Thank you. If you wouldn't mind taking me to the Amazon Hotel?" She'd purposely checked in there because it was near the Simonides building in the heart of the Plaka.

He nodded as he helped her in.

Before carrying out her plan to meet with Mr. Simonides today, Gabi had told her parents that one of her female coworkers from Alexandria, Virginia, was in Athens on a trip. They'd decided to get together and see a little of the sights. Gabi felt awful for outright lying to them, but she didn't dare let them know her true agenda.

Until Thea's fifth month of pregnancy when she'd developed serious heart complications and was hospitalized, Gabi hadn't even known the name of the babies' father. But as the end drew near and it became apparent Thea might not make it, she told Gabi to look in her jewel box at home and bring her the envelope she'd hidden there.

Gabi brought it to the hospital. Thea told her to open it. She took one look and gasped when she realized who the man was. "This is all I have of him. Like everyone else on board, we'd both had way too much to drink," Thea whispered. "We were 'strangers in the night' kind of thing."

Her confession elicited a moan from Gabi.

"It didn't mean anything to him. He didn't even know my name. I'm ashamed it happened and he shouldn't have to pay for a mistake which was as much mine as his. I wanted you to see him so you'll know what kind of genes the children have inherited. Now promise me you'll forget everything."

Gabi understood how Thea felt and planned to honor her wishes. Besides the unsuspecting father, she realized that any news would be exploited if linked to the Simonides family. As they had recently lost the daughter of her father's first marriage, Gabi wanted to save her parents any added grief.

While she sat there deep in thought the rear door opened. Surprised they'd already arrived in front of the hotel, she gave a start before getting out.

"Please thank your employer for me."

"Of course."

Once he'd gone, she hurried inside, anxious to eat something at the snack bar before going up to her room. Whatever Mr. Simonides intended to do, he was in the driver's seat and would be the one to set the timetable for their next conversation. *If there were to be one...*

She could only hope he would make the arrangements before morning. Tomorrow she needed to fly back to Heraklion on Crete and rejoin her family. On top of their sadness, they had their hands full with the twins who'd been born six weeks premature.

When it had looked as if Thea was in trouble, Gabi had taken an undetermined leave of absence from the advertising agency in Virginia to fly to Heraklion. Since then she'd taken over the care of the babies because her busy parents' demanding diplomatic position didn't allow for the constant nurturing of the twins without full-time help.

That was four months ago and Gabi's job as public relations manager had been temporarily filled by someone else at Hewitt and Wilson, so she had a vital decision to make. If Mr. Simonides chose to claim his children, then she needed to get back to her work in Virginia ASAP.

Her immediate boss had been made regional director of the East Coast market and hinted at an important promotion for her. But she needed to get back home if she wanted to expand her career opportunity with him. The only other career more important would be to become the mother to Thea's children. But if she chose to do that, then it meant she would have to give up her advertising career until they were school age.

Having been burned by Texas rancher and oil man Rand McCallister five years ago, Gabi had no intention of ever getting married or having children, but if the twins' birth father didn't want them, then she would take on the responsibility of raising them because they were her family. As such, she needed to go back to Virginia where she could rear them in familiar surroundings.

Her family's home in Alexandria was the perfect residence in a guarded, gated community with other diplomats' families, some of whom had small children. Gabi had always lived in it with her parents when they weren't in Greece on assignment. Since Gabi's father owned the house outright, she wouldn't have to deal with a mortgage payment.

If she combined the savings from her job with

her dad's financial help, she could be a stay-at-home mom until they were both school age, then get back to her career. It could all work. Gabi would *make* it work because she'd grown to love the twins as if they were her own babies.

In all likelihood Mr. Simonides wasn't interested in the children and had only made certain she got a ride back to wherever she'd come from. Therefore she would fly the twins to Alexandria with her next week.

After a quick meal, Gabi went up to her room on the fourth floor, reasoning that her mother would go with her to help the three of them settle in before returning to Crete. The consulate was no place for two new infants. Her parents would never admit it, but the whole situation had grown out of control.

No sooner did she let herself inside with the card key than she saw the red light blinking on the telephone. Her mother could have left a voice message rather than try to get her on her cell phone. Then again…

With an odd combination of curiosity and

trepidation, she reached for the receiver to retrieve it.

"Another limo is waiting for you in front of the hotel, Ms. Turner. It will be there until eight-thirty p.m." Her watch said eight-ten. "If you don't appear with your luggage by then, I'll understand this isn't a life and death situation after all. Your hotel-room bill has been taken care of."

Gabi hung up the phone feeling as if she were acting in a police procedural film, not living real life. He'd had her followed and watched. The fabulously wealthy Mr. Simonides inhabited a world made up of secrecy and bodyguards in order to preserve, not only his safety, but the privacy he craved.

She imagined the paparazzi constituted a living nightmare for him, particularly when someone unknown like Gabi materialized. Her intrusion reminded him there were consequences for a night of pleasure he couldn't remember because everyone partying on the yacht had been drinking heavily.

Thea had confided he was a Greek god come

to life. Unlike Gabi, who'd inherited her mother's shorter height and curves, Thea had been fashionably tall and thin. Growing up, she could have any boy she wanted.

She'd always had a man in tow, even the bachelor playboy Andreas Simonides touted in the press, now the crowned head of the Simonides empire. When he'd picked Thea out from the other women on board and had started making love to her in one of the cabins, she'd succumbed in a moment of extreme weakness.

How tragic that in celebrating her divorce she'd become pregnant, the consequences of which had brought on her death…

Gabi couldn't imagine Mr. Simonides forgetting her sister no matter what. But if he'd been like Rand, then there'd been many beautiful women in his life. As both sisters had learned, they'd only made up part of the adoring horde. What a huge shock it must have been to discover he'd fathered baby boys whose resemblance to the two of them was nothing short of astounding.

Gabi only had a few minutes to freshen up

and pack her overnight bag before she rushed down to the lobby. It was a simple matter since she hadn't planned to be in Athens more than a night and had only brought one other change of outfit with her.

Through the doors she spied a limo with dark glass, but a different driver stood next to it. She assumed she would be driven to an undisclosed location where Mr. Simonides was waiting for her.

"Good evening, Ms. Turner." He opened the rear door to help her in with her case. "I'll be taking you to Kyrie Simonides."

"Thank you."

Before long they were moving into the mainstream of heavy traffic circulating about the old Turkish quarter of Athens. Again she had the feeling she was playing a part in a movie, but this time she experienced a distinct chill because she'd dared to approach a complete stranger who had all the power.

The sky was darkening into night. If she were to disappear, her family wouldn't have a clue what had happened to her. Their pain at such an eventuality didn't bear thinking about. In the desire to unite the babies with their only living parent, she'd been blinded to the risks involved. Now it was too late to pull out of a possibly dangerous situation she'd created.

At this point she wasn't quite sure what she'd hoped to achieve. Unless a bachelor who partied and slept with women without giving it a thought were to give up that lifestyle, he wouldn't make the best father around. But for the sake of the twins who deserved more, she couldn't just take them back to Virginia and raise them without first trying to let their father know he *was* a father. Would he want any part in their lives?

She wanted him to be a real man and claim his children, invite them into his home and his life… be there for them for the whole of their lives. Give them his name and seal their legacy.

But of course that kind of thing just didn't happen. Gabi wasn't under any illusions. No doubt he was convinced she'd approached him to extort money and was ready to pay her off. He would soon find out she wanted nothing monetary from him and would be leaving for the States with her precious cargo.

Before Thea died, she'd asked Gabi to help get the babies placed for adoption with a good Greek couple. She wanted them raised Greek. Both sisters realized the impossible burden it would put on their older parents to shoulder the responsibility of raising the children. For all their sakes Gabi had made Thea that promise.

But after her death, Gabi realized it was a promise she couldn't keep. In the first place, the twins' birth father *was* alive. Legally no one could adopt them without his permission.

And in the second place, over the last three months Gabi had learned to love the boys. She'd bonded with them. Maybe she wasn't Greek, but, having been taught Greek from the cradle, Gabi was bilingual and would use it with them. They would have a good home with her. No one but their own father could ever pry them away from her now.

Suddenly the rear door opened. "Ms. Turner?" the driver called to her. "If you'll follow me."

Startled out of her thoughts, she exited the

limo, not having realized they'd arrived at the port of Piraeus. He held her overnight case and walked toward a gleaming white luxury cabin cruiser probably forty to forty-five feet in length moored a few steps away along the pier.

A middle-aged crew member took the bag and helped her aboard. "My name is Stavros. I'll take you to Kyrie Simonides, who's waiting for you to join him in the rear cockpit. This way, Ms. Turner."

Once again she found herself trailing after a stranger to an ultraleather wraparound lounge whose sky roof was open. Her dark-haired host was standing in front of the large windows overlooking the water lit up by the myriad boats and ferries lining the harbor. The dream vessel was state of the art.

Since she'd last seen him in the lift, he'd removed his suit jacket and tie. He'd rolled his shirtsleeves up to the elbow. Thea had been right. He was spectacular-looking.

She understood when the man announced to her host that the American woman had come aboard. He turned in her direction. The lights reflecting off the water cast his hard-boned features into stark relief.

"Come all the way in and sit down, Ms. Turner. Stavros will bring you anything you want to eat or drink."

"Nothing for me, thank you. I just ate."

After his staff member left the room, she pulled the envelope out of her purse and put it on the padded seat next to her, assuming he wanted a better look at everything. He wandered over to her, but made no move to take it. Instead his enigmatic gaze traveled over her upturned features.

She had an oval face, but her mouth was too wide and her hair was too naturally curly for her liking. Instead of olive skin, hers was a nondescript cream color. Her dad once told her she had wood violet eyes. She'd never seen wood violets, but he'd said it with such love, she'd decided that they were her one redeeming feature.

"My name's Andreas," he said, surprising her. "What's yours?"

"Gabi."

"My sources tell me you were christened

Gabriella. I like the shortened version."
Unexpectedly he reeked of the kind of virile
charm to turn any woman's head. Thea hadn't
stood a chance.

Gabi understood that kind of potent male
power and the money that went with it. Once
upon a time she'd loved Rand. Substitute this
Greek tycoon's trappings for seven hundred
thousand acres of Texas ranch land with cattle
and oil wells and voilà—the two men were
interchangeable. Fortunately for Gabi, she'd
only needed to learn her lesson once. Thea had
learned hers, too, but it had come at the cost of
her life.

One black brow quirked. "Where are these
twins? At your home in Virginia, or are they a
little closer at your father's consulate residence
in Heraklion?"

With a mere phone call he knew people in
the highest places to get that kind of classified
information in less than an hour. Naturally he
did. She wanted to tell him that, since he possessed all the facts, there was no need to answer

his question, but she couldn't do that. Not after she'd been the one to approach him.

"They're on Crete."

"I want to see them," he declared without hesitation, sending Gabi into mild shock that he'd become curious about these children who could be his offspring. She felt a grudging respect that he'd conceded to the possibility that his relationship with Thea, no matter how short-lived, had produced them. "How soon are you due back in Heraklion?"

"When I left this morning, I told my parents I was meeting a former work colleague from the States in Athens and would fly home tomorrow."

"Will they send a car for you?"

"No. I told them I wasn't sure of my arrival time so I'd take a taxi."

He shifted his weight. "Once I've delivered you to Heraklion, there'll be a taxi waiting to take you home. For the time being Stavros has prepared a room for you. Are you susceptible to the *mal de mer*?"

They were going back by sea?

"No."

"Good. I'm assuming your parents are still in the dark about the twins' father, otherwise you wouldn't have needed to lie to them."

"Thea never wanted them to know." She hadn't wanted anyone to know, especially not Thea's ex-husband Dimitri. For the most part their marriage had been wretched and she hadn't wanted him to find out what she'd done on the very day she'd obtained her divorce from him. Dimitri wouldn't hesitate to expose his ex-wife's indiscretion out of simple revenge.

"Yet she trusted *you*."

"Not until she knew she might die." Thea hadn't wanted to burden anyone. "Though she admitted making a mistake she dearly regretted, she wanted her babies to be taken care of without it being Mom and Dad's responsibility. I approached you the way I did in order to spare them and you any notoriety."

"But not my pocketbook," he inserted in a dangerously silken voice.

"You would have every right to think that, Mr. Simonides."

"Andreas," he corrected her.

She took a deep breath. "Money isn't the reason I came. Nor do you have to worry your name is on their birth certificates. Thea refused to name the father. Though I promised to find a good home for the twins with another couple, I couldn't keep it."

"Why not?"

"Because you're alive. I've looked into the law. No one can adopt them unless you give away your parental rights. In truth, Thea never wanted you to know anything."

He shrugged his elegant shoulders. "If not for money, then why didn't you just spirit them away and forget the legalities?"

Gabi stared hard at him. "Because I plan to adopt them and had to be certain you didn't want to claim them before I take them back to Virginia with me. You have that God-given right after all." She took a fortifying breath. "Being their aunt, I don't."

Her lids prickled, but she didn't let tears form. "As for the twins, they have the same God-given right to be with their father if you want *them*. If there was any chance of that happening, I had to take it, thus my presence in your office today. Naturally if you do want them, then I'll tell my parents everything and we'll go from there."

The air seemed to have electrified around them. "If you're telling me the truth, then you're one of a dying species."

His cynical remark revealed a lot. He had no qualms about using women. In that regard he and Rand had a lot in common. But Gabi suspected Mr. Simonides didn't like women very much.

"One day when they're old enough to understand, I wouldn't be able to face them if I couldn't tell them that at the very beginning I did everything in my power to unite them with you first."

His eyes looked almost black as they searched hers for a tension-filled moment. "What's in Virginia when your parents are here in Greece?"

"*My life*, Mr. Simonides. Like you, I have an important career I love. My parents' responsibilities are here on Crete for the time being. Dad has always had connections to the Greek government. Every time they're transferred, I make the occasional visit, but I live at our family home in Virginia."

"How long have you been here?"

"I came a month before the children were born. They're three months old now." *They're so adorable you can't imagine.*

"What's your routine with them?"

Gabi thought she understood what he was asking. "Between naps I usually take them for walks in their stroller."

"Where?"

"Several places close by. There's a small park with a fountain and benches around the corner from the consulate. I sometimes go there with them."

"Let's plan to meet there tomorrow, say three o'clock. If that isn't possible, phone me on my cell and we'll arrange for another time."

"That will be fine," she assured him.

"Good." He wrote a number on a business card and handed it to her. In the next breath he pulled the phone out of his trouser pocket and asked Stavros to report.

Half a minute later the other man appeared. "Come with me, Ms. Turner, and I'll show you to your cabin."

"Thank you." When she got up, she would have taken the envelope with her, but Andreas was too fast for her.

"I'll return this to you later. Let's hope you sleep well. The sea is calm tonight."

She paused at the entrance. Studying him from across the expanse she said, "Thank you for giving me those two minutes. When I prevailed on your receptionist, she said you were already late leaving your office. I'm sorry if I interrupted your plans for the evening."

He cocked his dark head. "A life and death situation waits on no man. Go to bed with a clear conscience. *Kalinihta*, Gabi Turner."

His deep, attractive voice vibrated to her insides. *"Kalinihta."*

As soon as Stavros saw her to her cabin, Andreas pulled out his cell phone to call Irena for the second time this evening.

"Darling?" she answered on the second ring. "I've been hoping to hear from you."

"I'm sorry about tonight," he began without preamble. "As I told you earlier, an emergency came up that made it impossible for us to join the family party on Milos."

"Well, you're free now. Are you planning to come over?"

He gripped the phone tighter. "I can't."

"That sounded serious. Something really is wrong, isn't it?"

"Yes," his voice grated. In the space of a few hours his shock had worn off enough for agony to take over.

"You don't want to talk to me about it?"

"I will when the time is right." He closed his eyes tightly. *There was no right time. Not for this.*

"Which means you have to discuss it with Leon first."

What did she just say?

"Judging by your silence, I realize that came out wrong. Forgive me. Ever since we started seeing each other, I've learned you always turn to him before anyone else, but I said it as an observation, not a criticism."

She'd only spoken the truth. It brought up a potentially serious issue for the future, but he didn't have the time to analyze the ramifications right now. "There's nothing to forgive, Irena. I'll call you tomorrow."

"Whatever's disturbing you, remember I'm here."

"As if I could forget."

"*S'agapo*, Andreas."

In the six months they'd been together, he'd learned to love her. Before Gabi Turner had come to his office, he'd planned to ask Irena to marry him. It was past time he settled down. His intention had been to announce it at tonight's party.

"*S'agapo,*" he whispered before hanging up.

CHAPTER TWO

THE next afternoon Gabi's mother helped her settle the babies in their double stroller. "It's hot out."

"A typical July day." Gabi had already packed their bottled formula in the space behind the seat. "I've dressed them in their thinnest tops and shorts." One outfit in pale green, the other pastel blue. "At least there's some shade at the park. We'll have a wonderful time, won't we?"

She couldn't resist kissing their cheeks. After being gone overnight, she'd missed them horribly. Now that they were awake, their sturdy little arms and legs were moving like crazy.

"Oh, Gabi…they're so precious and they look so much like Thea."

"I know." But they also looked like someone else. That was the reason they were so gorgeous. She squeezed her mother around the shoulders. "Because of them, Thea will always be with us."

"Your father's so crazy about them, I don't know if he can handle your taking them back home to Alexandria to live. I know I can't. Please promise me you'll reconsider."

"We've been over this too many times, Mom. Dad can't do his work the way he needs to. It's best for both of you with your busy schedules. At home I'll be around my friends and there'll be other moms with their babies to befriend. We'll see each other often. You know that!"

Right now Gabi had too many butterflies in her stomach at the thought of meeting up with Andreas to concentrate on anything else. She slowly let go of her. "See you later."

Making certain the twins were comfy, she started pushing the stroller away from the Venetian-styled building that had become a home to the consulate with its apartments for their family. From her vantage point she could look out over the port of Heraklion on the north-

ern end of Crete, an island steeped in Roman
and Ottoman history.

Normally she daydreamed about its past
during her walks with the children, but this
afternoon her gaze was glued to the harbor.
Somewhere down there was the cabin cruiser
that had brought her from Piraeus.

The trip had been so smooth, she could believe the sea had been made of glass. She should
have fallen into a deep sleep during the all-night
crossing, but in truth she'd tossed and turned
most of it.

That was because the man she'd labeled blood-
less and selfish didn't appear to fit her original
assessment. In fact she had trouble putting him
in any category, which was yet another reason
for her restlessness.

As a result she'd slept late and had to be
awakened by Stavros, who'd brought a fabulous breakfast to her elegant cabin with its
cherrywood décor. She'd thanked him profusely.
Following that she'd showered and given herself
a shampoo. After drying her hair, she'd changed

into white sailor pants and a sleeveless navy and white print top.

Once her bag was packed, she'd applied lipstick, then walked through to the main salon before ascending the companionway stairs in her sandals. She'd expected to find Andreas so she could thank him for everything, but discovered he was nowhere in sight. Somehow she'd felt disappointed, which made no sense at all.

Since Stavros had let her know her ride was waiting, she'd had no choice but to leave the cruiser from the port side. He'd carried her overnight bag to the taxi and wished her a good day. After thanking him again, she'd been whisked through the bustling city of close to a hundred and forty thousand people. Further up the incline they reached the consulate property and passed through the sentry gate.

After her arrival, she'd made some noncommittal remarks to her parents about having had an okay time in Athens, but she'd missed the children too much and wanted to come straight home. The babies had acted so happy to see her, her heart had melted.

Closer to the park now, she felt her pulse speed up. Though the heat had something to do with it, there was another reason. What if Andreas took one look and decided he *did* want the children? Though that was what she'd been hoping and praying for, she hadn't counted on this pang that ran through her at the thought of having to give them up.

The park held its share of children, some with their mothers. A few older people sat on benches talking. Several tourists on bikes had stopped to catch their breath before moving on. It was a benign scene until she noticed the striking man who sat beneath the fronds of a palm tree reading a newspaper.

There was an aura of sophistication about him. A man in control of his world. One of the most powerful men in Greece actually. Everywhere he went, his bodyguards preceded him, but she would never know who they were or where they were hidden.

Today he'd dressed in a silky blue sport shirt and tan trousers, a picture of masculine strength and a kind of rugged male beauty hard to put in words.

She glanced at the twins. They didn't know it, but they were looking at their daddy, a man like no other who wasn't more than ten feet away.

His intelligent eyes fringed with inky black lashes peered over the newspaper at them before he put it aside and stood up.

Gabi moved the stroller closer until they were only a few feet apart. Hardly able to breathe, she touched one dark, curly head. "This is Kris, short for Kristopher. And this..." she tousled the other gleaming cap of black curls "...is Nikos."

Andreas hunkered down in front of them. Like finding a rare treasure, his eyes burned a silvery gray as his gaze inspected every precious centimeter, from their handsome faces to the tips of their bare toes.

He cupped their chins as if he were memorizing their features, then he let them wrap their fingers around his. Before long both his index fingers ended up in their mouths.

Gabi started to laugh. She couldn't help it.

"He tastes good, huh. You little guys must be hungry." She undid the strap and handed Nikos to him. "Sit down on the bench and you can feed him." In a flash she supplied him with a cloth against his shoulder and a baby bottle full of formula.

"If you've never done this before, don't worry about it. The boys will do all the work. Let him drink for a minute, then pat his back gently to get rid of the air bubbles. I'll take care of Kris."

For the next little while, she was mostly aware of the twins making noisy sounds as they drank their bottles with the greatest of relish. Afterward they traded babies so he could get to know Kris.

Every so often the sounds were followed by several loud burps that elicited rich laughter from Andreas. When she'd approached him in his office yesterday, she hadn't thought he was capable of it.

Any misgivings she'd had about starting up this process fled at the sight of him getting acquainted with the boys. It was a picture that would be impressed on her heart forever.

Wherever Thea was, she had to be happy her sons were no longer strangers to their father, even if he'd never sought her sister out again.

Gabi didn't know the outcome, but this meeting was something to cherish at least.

"We'll have to make this fast because I don't want to keep them out in the sun much longer." She flashed him a quick glance. "Next time—if you want there to be a next time—you can take them for a walk on your own."

He made no response. She didn't know what to think. Another five minutes passed before she said, "There now. They're as sated as two fat cats." Again she heard laughter roll out of him.

Together they lowered them back into the stroller. Her arm brushed his, making her unduly aware of him. She put the empty bottles and cloths away. When she rose up, their glances collided. "I have to go," she said. Maybe she was mistaken, but she thought the light in his eyes faded a trifle. "If you want to see them again, call me on my cell."

Pulling out his phone, he said, "Tell me your

number and I'll program it into mine right now."

Maybe that was a good sign. Then again maybe it wasn't. A small shiver ran down her spine in fear that when he contacted her next, he would tell her that, cute as the boys were, he was still signing his rights away and they were all hers with his blessing.

After she'd given him her number, he pushed the stroller toward the path leading out to the street. One of the older women caught sight of the twins and shouted something about them having beautiful children.

"*Efharisto,*" Andreas called back, thanking the woman as if this were an everyday occurrence.

Gabi didn't want to tear herself away, but her mother would worry if she wasn't back soon and would want to know why the delay. "I really have to go."

"I know," he said in a husky tone before giving the boys a kiss on their foreheads. "I'll be in touch."

With those long powerful strides, he left the

park going one way while she trundled along with the stroller going the other. The farther apart they got, the more fearful she grew.

He wasn't indifferent to the twins. She knew that. She'd felt it and seen it. But one meeting with his children didn't mean he wanted to take on the lifetime responsibility of parenting them. Between his work and girlfriends he wouldn't have much time to fit in the twins.

She'd told him she'd be leaving for Virginia next week. If he didn't want her to take them away, he needed to make up his mind soon.

Maybe he would compromise. She'd raise them and he'd be one of those drop-in daddies. For the boys' sake Gabi couldn't bear the thought of it, but having a daddy around once in a while, even if he only flew into D.C. from Greece once a year with a present, was better for them than no daddy at all, wasn't it? Gabi loved her own father so much, she couldn't imagine life without him.

The only thing to do now was brace herself for his next phone call.

* * *

Accompanied by his bodyguards, Andreas rushed toward the helicopter waiting for him at the Heraklion airport. Once he'd climbed aboard, he directed his pilot to fly him to the Simonides villa on Milos where the whole clan had congregated for the weekend.

Last night there'd been a party to celebrate his sister Melina's thirtieth birthday, but he'd been forced to miss it because of a life and death situation. *Gabi Turner had been right about that.*

Though his married sister had been gracious over the phone, he knew she'd been hurt by his excuse that something unavoidable had come up to detain him in Athens. He'd promised to make it up to her, but that kind of occasion in her honor with extended family in attendance only happened once a year. Now the moment was gone.

Yet, sorry as he was, he had something much more vital on his mind and couldn't think about anything else. Throughout the flight he still felt the strong tug of those little mouths on his fingers. Their touch had sent the most peculiar sensation through Andreas.

Even though he had ten nieces and nephews, he hadn't been involved in their nurturing. The closest he'd come was to hold their weightless bodies as they were being passed around at a family party after coming home from the hospital.

Today had been something totally different. It was as if the blinders had come off, but he hadn't known they existed until contact was made. Kris and Nikos weren't just babies. Those excited bodies with their bright eyes and faces belonged to a pair of little guys who one day would grow up to be big guys. Guys who had the Simonides stamp written all over them.

As soon as he entered the main villa Andreas went in search of his vivacious mother, who was in the kitchen supervising dinner preparations with the cook, Tina.

"There you are, darling," she said the minute she saw him.

He gave her a kiss, already anticipating her next comment. "My absence was unavoidable."

Her expressive dark brows lifted. "A delicate merger?"

"Incredibly delicate," he muttered. The memory of Nikos and Kris so trusting in his arms as they inhaled their formula never left his mind.

"You sound like your father. I have to tell you I'm glad he's finally stepped down and you're in charge. He's a different man these days. Let's just hope that when you're settled down, hopefully soon, your wife will have more influence on you to take time off once in a while. You're already working too hard if you had to miss Melina's birthday party."

His mother could have no idea. He gave her an extra hug. "Where's everyone?" he asked, knowing the answer full well, but he didn't want to sound like anything out of the ordinary was wrong.

"Still waterskiing. Your grandparents are out on the patio watching your father and your uncle Vasio drive the younger children around. We'll eat out by the pool in an hour."

"That gives me enough time to get in a little exercise." After stealing an hors d'oeuvre from the plate Tina was preparing, he pecked her cheek to atone for his sin before walking through a series of alcoves and walkways to reach his villa with its own amenities farther down their private beach.

The massive family retreat—a cluster of linked white villas in the Cycladic style—had been the Simonides refuge for many generations. Because of business, Andreas didn't escape from his penthouse in the city as often as he wanted and had been looking forward to this time with the family.

Who would have dreamed that, before the lift door closed, an innocent-looking blonde female would sweep into his office like a Cycladic breeze, bringing a fragrance as sweet as the honeysuckle growing wild on the island before she dropped her bomb?

Still charged with adrenaline, he changed into his swim trunks and hurried down to the beach where the family ski boats were in use.

"There's Uncle Andreas!" One of his nieces waiting on the beach for her turn screeched with joy and ran toward him. Her brother followed. "Now that you're here, will you take us? Grandpa hasn't come back for us yet."

His sister Leila's children were the youngest, seven and nine. "What do *you* think?" He grinned. "Climb in my ski boat. We'll show everybody! You spot your sister first, Jason."

"Okay!"

Happy chaos reigned for another half-hour, then everyone left the beach because dinner had been announced. Andreas secured his boat to their private pier. Things couldn't have turned out better than to find his brother Leon the last to tie up his own ski boat. His wife Deline had gone up with the others, leaving them alone for the moment.

"How was the party last night?" Andreas asked as he started tying the other end for him.

Leon shot him a glance. "Fine, but I have to tell you Dad wasn't too thrilled you didn't make a showing. He was hoping to see you there with Irena."

Irena Liapis was a favorite with the family and the daughter of his parents' good friends who owned one of the major newspapers in Greece. It was the same paper that had shown Thea aboard the family yacht.

Everyone was hoping for news that a wedding was in the offing. With his four siblings married, his parents were expecting some kind of announcement from him.

Andreas groaned. No woman had ever been his grand passion. Maybe there wasn't such a thing and he was only deluding himself because he'd been a bachelor for too long. But his feelings for Irena had grown over the months. Besides being beautiful, she was intelligent and kind. He wanted his marriage to work and knew it could if she were his wife.

But last night Gabi Turner's explosion into his life had caused every plan to go up in smoke. Now that a certain situation had developed threatening to set off a conflagration, his whole world had been turned on its side. For the time being he couldn't think about Irena or anything else.

Andreas knew it wasn't fair to keep any secrets from the woman he'd intended to marry, but, as he'd just found out, life wasn't fair…not to the twins who'd lost their mother or to Gabi who'd taken on the awesome responsibility of raising her half sister's children.

By tacit agreement he and his brother started walking up the beach toward the pool area. Using his fingertips, Leon scooped up his sandals lying in the sand. "Your non-appearance was kind of a shocker. Normally Dad gives you a pass."

"It's because he has a soft spot for Melina." She was the baby in the family.

"If you pulled off the Canadian gold-refining merger, I'm sure all will be forgiven."

Andreas frowned. "That might not happen. I'm still debating if it's to our advantage."

"With the kind of revenue it could bring in, you must be joking!"

"Not at all. I think they're in deeper trouble than they've made out to be." He gave his brother a covert glance. "Speaking of trouble, there's something you and I have to talk about in private."

"If you're referring to the acquisition of those mineral rights in—"

"I'm not," he cut him off. "You made a brilliant move on that." Leon was his second in command. "I'm referring to something else that doesn't have anything to do with business. After we eat, come to my villa alone. Make it look casual. You need to see something."

Leon let out a bark of laughter. "You sound cryptic. What's gotten into you?"

"You'll find out soon enough."

For the next hour Andreas joined in with his family and gave Melina the gift he'd found for her on one of his business trips to the Balkans. She collected nesting dolls. The one he gave her proved to be a hit. Once dessert was served, he faded from the scene and headed for his place, nodding to one of the maids on the way. Not long after, Leon showed up.

"Lock the front door behind you. I don't want us to be disturbed."

Leon flicked him a puzzled glance as he pushed in the button. He walked into the living room. "What's going on? The last time I remember seeing you this intense was when Father suffered that mild heart attack last year."

Heart attack was the operative word.

Andreas was still trying to recover from the one Ms. Turner had given him. Without wasting any more time he handed the newspaper photo to Leon, who studied it for a minute before lifting his head. "Why are you showing me a picture of you? I don't understand." He handed it back to him.

"If you'll notice the date, this headline is a year old. When the picture was taken, I happened to be in the States on business with our big brother. As usual, the paparazzi got you and me mixed up. That was during the time you and Deline were separated. This tall, raven-haired beauty who's looking over at you was the woman, right?"

Only now did it strike Andreas that Thea bore a superficial resemblance to both Deline and Irena. Sometimes it astounded him that he and Leon had similar tastes, not only in certain kinds of foods and sports, but in women. They were all striking brunettes.

"Yes," he whispered. "And if I hadn't gone to Deline and told her the truth about that night, it could have cost me my marriage. I still marvel that she forgave me enough to give us a second chance."

Leon unexpectedly grabbed the paper out of his hand and balled it up in his fist. "Why are you reminding me of it? Look here, Andreas—" His cheeks had grown ruddy with unaccustomed anger.

"I *have* been looking," he came back in a quiet voice. "Because I love you and Deline, for the last twenty-four hours I've been doing whatever it takes to protect you and keep this news confidential."

"What do you mean?"

"I thought you'd like to know the name of the woman you spent that hour with on the yacht. Her name was Thea Paulos, the divorced daughter of Richard Turner, of the Greek-American Consulate on Crete. Her ex-husband Dimitri Paulos is the son of Ari Paulos who owns Paulos Metal Exports, one of the subsidiary companies we acquired a few years ago."

While his brother stood there swallowing hard, Andreas removed the twins' photo and DNA results from the manila envelope and handed everything to him.

Stunned into silence, Leon sank down on the couch to stare at the children he'd unknowingly produced. Though Andreas had it in his heart to feel sorry for his brother's predicament, a part of him thought Leon the luckiest man on earth to have fathered two such beautiful sons.

"I had our DNA compared to theirs. It's a match."

Leon's face went white.

"I've seen them," Andreas confided. Thanks to Gabi, he'd held and fed both of them, an experience he'd never forget.

His brother's dark head reared back. "You've *seen* them—" He sounded incredulous.

"Yes. They're three months old."

"Three months?" He mouthed the words, obviously in shock. "How did Ms. Paulos contact you?"

"She didn't. Tragically for the children, she

died on the operating table giving birth to them."

"She's dead?" He kept repeating everything Andreas said, like a man in a trance.

"It was her half sister, Gabi Turner, who came to my office yesterday. She's the one who arranged for me to see the boys at a park near the consulate today."

His brother jumped up from the couch looking like a caged animal ready to spring.

"Take it easy, Leon. I know what you're thinking, but you'd be dead wrong. In the first place, she believes *I'm* the father."

Leon jerked around. "You didn't tell her *I* was the one in that news photo?"

"No."

His brother averted his eyes. "How much money does she want to keep quiet?" he asked in a subdued voice.

It was a fair question since the same one had dominated Andreas's thoughts when she'd first pulled out the photograph. "Forget about her desire to blackmail me. This has to do with something else entirely."

"And you believed her?" Leon cried, grabbing his shoulders.

Andreas supposed Gabi could have been lying through her teeth. If that were the case… He saw black for a moment before a semblance of reason returned.

"I'd stake my life on the fact that her only agenda for coming to me was to make sure I knew I had two sons before she left Greece."

"Why would she do that?"

He sucked in his breath. "Because she said they deserve to be with their real father if it's at all possible."

Leon's eyes clouded for a moment before he flashed Andreas a jaded look and released him. "It could be a ploy. Where's she supposedly going?"

"Alexandria, Virginia." To her home and her life, as she'd put it. "Her father started his diplomatic career there. I have confirmation of it."

While Leon stood there tongue tied, Andreas's cell phone rang. He checked the caller ID and clicked on. "Mother?"

"Where are you?"

"In my villa." He glanced at his brother. "Leon's with me."

"Can't you two stop talking business for one evening?"

"Yes. We'll be right over."

"Good. Everyone's wondering where you are. Deline's been looking everywhere. We're going to start some family movies."

"Tell her we're coming," Leon called out loud enough for her to hear before Andreas clicked off.

He went into the study and locked the envelope in his desk, then eyed his brother soberly. "Since Gabi thinks I'm the father, we'll leave it that way for now."

As soon as Leon handed the wad to him he set it in an ashtray on the coffee table and put a match to it. When the evidence was gone, he lifted his head. "Before you make a decision about anything, you need to see the twins for yourself."

Another odd sound escaped his brother.

"I'll phone Gabi and see if we can't arrange it for Monday. We'll make up some excuse to the family about a business emergency. We won't have to be gone long."

Leon buried his face in his hands. "How am I going to be able to act like everything's normal until then?"

A shudder passed through Andreas's body. "We're both going to have to find a way."

His dark head reared back. "When Deline finds out about this... I swear I've been doing everything to make our marriage work. It only happened that one time, Andreas. It'll never happen again. I love Deline." The tremor in his voice was real enough.

"I believe you."

"You know the reason why we separated for those two months. We'd been fighting over my working too much. She got on that old rant about my being married to you instead of her. She said she was tired of being neglected and told me I was the reason we hadn't gotten pregnant yet.

"When she told me she wanted a separation because she needed time to think, I was in hell. After weeks of trying to get her to talk to me, she told me she was thinking of making the separation permanent. I was so hurt, I ended up taking the yacht out. Some of my friends came along and brought women. There was too much drinking. I never meant to lose my head."

Andreas had heard it all before. He'd seen his brother was in anguish then, but this news added a terrifying new wrinkle.

After pacing the floor, Leon stopped and faced Andreas. "I know that was no excuse for making the ghastliest mistake of my life." His mouth formed a thin line. "Sorry you got involved in this mess." There was a lengthy pause. "It isn't your problem. It's *mine*, but I don't know what the hell I'm going to do about it yet."

At least Leon had admitted responsibility. "Once you've seen those babies, you'll figure it out." Of course Andreas could tell himself that now, but there was no sure way to know how his brother would feel after he'd gotten a look at them. "Let's agree that for the moment there's nothing else to be done. You go on back and find Deline. I'll be there in a few minutes."

Though he'd promised his mother he wouldn't be long, he found he didn't want to put off the phone call to Gabi until tomorrow. It surprised him how much he was looking forward to talking to her again.

Gabi had just finished changing the last diaper of the night when she heard her cell phone ring. She'd kept it in her jeans pocket to be certain she'd didn't miss Andreas's call if it came.

A peek at the caller ID and a rush of pleasure filled her body. Since her parents had gone out to dinner with guests, she could talk freely and clicked on.

"Andreas?"

"Good evening," came his deep, compelling voice. She liked the sound of it. Thea had obviously found it attractive, too. The knowledge that she'd had an intimate relationship with him increased Gabi's guilt and anger at herself for having any thoughts or feelings about him.

"Am I calling at the wrong moment?"

"No." She left the bedroom that had been turned into a nursery and closed the door. "It's a perfect time." Gabi was the only person to speak for the children. He sounded eager enough to see them again. "The children are finally down until their three-o'clock bottle, thank heaven."

"Then you're going to need your beauty sleep, so I won't keep you."

She let the remark pass. His only agenda had to do with his children, who appeared to be growing on him. That was the result she'd been hoping for. Leaning against the wall in the hall, she said, "Have you decided you want to see the twins again?"

"Yes. Could we meet at the park on Monday?"

Her pulse sped up. "Of course. When would you like to come? Morning or afternoon is fine with me."

"Morning would be an ideal time for me."

"Then I'll meet you at ten o'clock. After they've been fed and had their baths, I often take them on a walk when it's not so hot."

"I'm anxious to see them again."

That was an excellent sign. "The children love any attention." Especially when it was from their father. "I'll see you then."

"Gabi?" There was a nuance in his voice that caught her off guard.

"Yes?"

She heard him take a deep breath. "Thank you for being there for them."

It was too early for her to get a handle on his vision for their future. After his visit on Monday to see the children, there might not be another one. She had to prepare herself for that possibility. "You don't need to thank me. I wouldn't be anywhere else."

"I've noticed you don't accept compliments graciously, so I'll say it another way. Not everyone would do what you're doing. Not for your sister, not for anyone."

"Before you give me too much credit, don't forget I watched the twins being born. It was a life-changing experience for me."

"I don't doubt it. *Ta Leme.*" She knew that phrase well enough.

Gabi hung up, wishing his visit was as soon as tomorrow instead of Monday. She would like to know his plans because she was leaving with the children next week. It was no good staying in Greece any longer. One way or the other, she needed to get on with her life and her parents needed to get on with theirs.

During Gabi's morning walk with the children, Kris had nodded off. Last night he'd played too hard after she'd gotten up to give him a bottle. Nikos, on the other hand was wide awake and raring to go.

When she reached the park bench beneath the shade, she undid the strap and picked him up. He clung to her as she showed him the fountain. The noise of the babbling water had captured his attention. She looked round to see if Kris was all right. As before, her breath caught to discover Andreas standing over the stroller looking down at him.

Every time she saw the boys' father, she experienced a guilty rush of excitement that was impossible to smother. He'd dressed in a light blue business suit with a darker blue shirt and no tie, the personification of male splendor in her eyes. Thea's, too.

There was a time when Gabi hadn't thought there was a man who came close to Rand in his cowboy boots and Stetson. While on her two-week summer vacation with Rachel McCallister, her friend from college, she'd fallen hard for Rachel's cousin and his Texas charm. Two weeks of a whirlwind relationship and she'd thought it would go on forever.

Too late she found out there was nothing deeper to back up his fascinating drawl and the smile in those dancing blue eyes. He'd let her go back to Alexandria without making any kind of plans to see her again. When she learned through Rachel that he was getting married to his old girlfriend, Gabi's heart withered.

Since then she'd met and dated some attractive, successful men at her work and at the consulate, but she took no relationship seriously. Her career had become her top priority, the one thing she could count on.

Thankfully she'd learned her lesson well before meeting the legendary Andreas Simonides. Though there was no male to equal his intelligence or incredible appeal, she wouldn't fall into that trap again. Once had been enough.

She walked toward him carrying Nikos. "Good morning."

"*Kalimera.*" His voice had a lazy, almost seductive quality. She felt his gaze linger on her face before he switched his attention to Nikos. Again his gray eyes lit up. "Do you remember me?" He kissed the baby's cheek.

Nikos's eyelids fluttered in reaction. He was so cute.

"Gabi?" His eyes trapped hers once more. They held a trace of anxiety. "I brought someone with me I'd like you to meet."

Who?

Maybe it was a woman he was thinking of marrying now that he was running the Simonides company. Gabi fought to remain calm. Naturally that woman would be hopelessly in love with him. But when she learned he had two sons, would she be able to accept and eventually love the children he'd fathered with someone else?

Suddenly Gabi was feeling very possessive. No woman could mother them the way she could, but it was none of her business since she had no parental claim to the boys.

He put a hand on her upper arm and squeezed gently. "It's all right," he whispered, noticing how quiet she'd gone. "I trust him with my life."

Him?

While her heart picked up the lost beat, Andreas stepped around the end of the wall. Within two seconds he came back again, but at this point Gabi thought her vision had become blurred because she was looking at two of Andreas.

She blinked in alarm, but nothing seemed to clear her double vision. They came closer, in range now, she realized there was nothing wrong with her eyesight. Moving toward her was Andreas and his mirror image wearing a tan suit and cream shirt, only he didn't have a scar and his hair was the same style and longer length as in the news photo.

Gabi stared at Andreas in surprise. "You're a *twin!*"

"That's right. Gabriella Turner, meet my best friend and older brother by five minutes, Leonides Simonides."

"Hello, Mr. Simonides," she said, shaking his hand.

"Leon? Say hello to your sons."

CHAPTER THREE

Thea had been with Leonides Simonides, not Andreas?

"Ms. Turner? I hardly know what to say." Leon looked as stunned as she felt. In fact he barely got those words out because his gaze had fastened on the boys in visible disbelief.

"Gabi's holding Nikos," Andreas stated, filling in the silence. "Down there is Kris, who looks like he just woke up from his catnap."

Swift as the speed of light Andreas caught Gabi's eye and winked. Warmth flowed through her body as she smiled back, remembering the humorous comment she'd made on Saturday about the children being fat cats.

But she couldn't forget Leon. Though Andreas would have told him about the children ahead of time, this still had to be the most earthshaking moment of his life. She wasn't surprised he sank down on the bench literally stupefied.

"Would you like to hold Nikos?" she asked.

"I won't know what to do if he cries," he murmured, ashen faced.

"He won't." She handed the baby to him. By now Andreas had reached for Kris and was kissing his sweet little neck.

Deciding to give them privacy, she wandered to the other side of the park and sat down to finish reading the biography she'd picked up on the life of the French chef Julia Child.

She hadn't enjoyed a book as good as this in several years. Like Julia, Gabi had experienced an epiphany about food. But it hadn't happened until her father had been transferred to Crete where she'd tasted her first *pastitsio* and developed an instant love of Greek cuisine.

During the last few months she'd been practicing in the kitchen at the consulate, determined she would raise the boys on Greek food in honor of both their parents. By now she could make pretty good *spanakopita*.

When she realized she'd read the next page for

the tenth time, she closed the book and looked across the park. The babies had been put back in the stroller. Both men stood next to them. It seemed as if Andreas was doing most of the talking. Gabi wasn't sure what it all meant.

Hesitant to interrupt, she waited until he started wheeling the stroller toward her with a grave countenance marring his handsome features. She put the book back in her purse and stood up, noticing that Leon had walked out to the street.

"Let me apologize for my brother." He spoke without preamble.

"There's no need. It's not every day a man is confronted by instant fatherhood, especially when they're twins." The happiness she'd felt earlier to see the children united with Andreas had dissipated. Not in her wildest dreams would she have thought up a contingency where his twin brother was the father!

Andreas eyed her with a solemn expression. "Especially when he's been married three years."

A small gasp escaped her throat. Had Thea

known he was married, or hadn't it mattered to either of them in the heat of the moment?

"Obviously he's going to need some time," she whispered.

"You're a very understanding woman. When he can gather his wits, I'm sure he'll want to talk to you." She was fairly certain Leon wouldn't, particularly when Andreas would have already told him she planned to go home to Virginia and raise the twins. But she didn't say anything.

"Thank you for making this meeting today possible, Gabi."

It sounded like a goodbye speech if she'd ever heard one. Leon had probably told him he couldn't deal with the situation. What man could? One night in a stranger's arms wasn't supposed to end up like this. He wouldn't be the first father to opt out of his responsibilities.

She felt sorry for Andreas, who clearly loved his brother and had done everything he could to support him. "Of course. I approached *you*, remember? Thanks to you I won't ever have to lie to the children."

After clearing her throat, she said, "When I

get back to Virginia, I'll be reconnecting the phone and will leave the new phone number on a voice mail for you. That way if your brother ever wants to contact me, you can give him both numbers. One last thing. Please let him know I'll never try to get hold of him for any reason."

His eyes turned as black as his grim expression. "How soon are you leaving?" he asked in a gravelly voice.

"The day after tomorrow." She extended her hand, not wanting to prolong the inevitable. "Goodbye, Mr. Simonides."

Tuesday evening Gabi's phone alerted her to a text message while she was packing the last of the babies' clothes into the big suitcase. Her parents were in the nursery playing with the twins, their last night together for two months or more. Pretty soon it would be bedtime. Her dad wanted to put them down.

Since yesterday when she'd pushed the stroller in the opposite direction from Andreas and his brother, she'd tried hard to put the whole business behind her. She thought she'd been doing a fairly good job of hiding her feelings from her parents. Any pain they'd seen would have been attributed to tomorrow's dreaded departure.

Little did they know she'd met the boys' father. To her dismay he was doing nothing to prevent her from taking his children out of the country, out of his life.

Gabi hurt for his sons.

She hurt so horribly she could scarcely bear it, but she had to handle it because that was her agreement with Andreas. She would honor her commitment even if it was killing her.

With a tortured sigh she reached for the phone on the dresser. Her best friend Jasmin knew she was coming home and probably wanted to find out her flight number and time. But when she saw who'd sent the message, her adrenaline kicked in, causing her heart to thud.

I just arrived in Heraklion. When you've put the twins to bed, meet me at the park. I'll wait till morning if I have to because we need to talk. A.

She had to stifle her cry of joy. This meant Leon had been having second thoughts about letting his children slip away without making some arrangement to see them again. It meant she would have contact with Andreas one more time. Gabi wished her pulse didn't race faster at the thought.

After shutting the suitcase, she hurried to her bedroom to change. She slipped off her T-shirt and jeans, then reached for the tan pleated pants and kelly green cotton top she'd left out to wear on the plane tomorrow.

Once she'd run the brush through her curls and put on lipstick, she poked her head around the door of the nursery. Her parents were absorbed with the children, too busy to be unduly curious about her. "I'm going out for a few minutes to pick up some things at the store."

"Don't be too long," her dad cautioned in between singing to Nikos off-key. The scene melted her heart.

"I won't."

A minute later she waved to the guard at the sentry and headed in the direction of the park.

Because of the reflection from the water, twilight brought out the beauty of the Greek islands, but never more so than tonight. It was Andreas's fault. The knowledge he was waiting for her had added that magical quality.

Maybe this was how Thea had felt when she'd met Leon that evening aboard the yacht, as if the heavens were close for a moment and one of the twin gods from Olympus had come near enough for a human to touch.

He'd come close all right, so close he'd touched her with two little mortals, and now his twin, the powerful god Andreas, was here to parlay a deal between the two worlds. When Gabi thought of him in that light, the stars left her eyes and sanity returned.

Tonight he wasn't dressed like a god. She spied him at the fountain wearing a cream sport shirt and khakis. No one else was about. Instead of expensive hand-sewn leather shoes, he'd worn sandals like everyone else walking along the beachfront.

He watched her coming, but didn't make a move toward her. "*Yassou*, Gabi."

"Hi!" *Keep it airy.* "I came the minute I got your message because Mother and I have an early morning flight to Athens."

"I'm aware of that." He stood with his hands on his hips, emanating a stunning male virility. "Before you go anywhere, I have something in mind I'd like to discuss with you."

She blinked. "Why isn't Leon with you?"

Andreas studied her for a long moment. "I think you know the answer to that question."

Gabi was afraid she did, but Andreas's presence confused her. "Then I don't understand why *you're* here."

"Because I don't want you to leave Greece."

She struggled to stifle her moan. Of all the things he might have said, his blunt answer wasn't even on her list. Now if Rand had said, "I don't want you to leave Austin…" But he hadn't said anything. As for Andreas, she knew his agenda had nothing to do with her personally.

"I don't understand."

He took a deep breath. "Leon's in a panic right now, but in another day or two he's going to conquer it. When he does, the children need to be here, not clear across the Atlantic."

Gabi was the one starting to panic and shook her head. "I can't stay on Crete."

His pewter gaze pierced her. "Why not?"

"B-because my parents need to get their life back," she stammered. "The boys and I need our own home."

He took a step closer. "You've had a home here for months. I would imagine your parents will be devastated when the babies are gone. Therefore that couldn't be the real reason you're so anxious to take flight. Do you have a lover in Alexandria waiting for you?"

Taking the out he'd proffered, she said, "As a matter of fact I do. Not that it's anyone's business." While she spoke, she watched a young couple who'd wandered into the park and had started kissing.

"You're lying. Otherwise he'd have flown here to whisk you and the children back to Virginia weeks ago." The comment had come out more like a soft hiss. He would make a terrifying adversary if crossed.

She turned her eyes away from the amorous couple. "If you must know, I want the children to myself."

"So they'll know you're their mother," he deduced. "That makes perfect sense, but you don't have to go to Virginia to do that."

Gabi sucked in her breath. "I don't have the means to earn a living right now and Dad's home in Alexandria is paid for. With my savings and his financial help, it will work until they're in school and I can go to work."

He shook his dark head. "I've learned enough to know your father has the means to help you move into your own place here on Crete where you and the boys can be close by but still independent. Why are you afraid to tell me the truth? What's going on?"

Andreas saw too much. "There are already too many questions being asked about the paternity of the twins. My parents don't know anything. If it got out about your brother and Thea, my family as well as yours would suffer and you know it. That's why I want to take them back with me."

"Out of sight, out of mind, you mean."

"Yes."

He rubbed the back of his neck. "That might work for a while, but it's inevitable the day will arrive when the secret comes out. They always do. By then the damage will be far worse, not only for the families involved but for the twins themselves."

"I realize that, but for the present I don't know what else to do. There's—" She stopped herself in time, but Andreas immediately picked up on it.

"What were you going to say?"

"N-nothing."

"Tell me!" he demanded.

Feeling shaky, she said, "I should never have come to your office."

"That isn't what you were about to blurt."

The man had radar. At this point she had no choice but to tell him. Not everything, but enough to satisfy him.

Taking a few steps, she sank down on the park bench. He followed, but stood near her with his tanned fingers curled around the back railing.

"Thea's husband would love to hurt our family for backing her in the divorce. He's capable of making trouble that could make things unpleasant for Leon, too."

"You're talking about Dimitri Paulos."

Gabi got up from the bench. "How did you know?"

His eyes played over her. "I did a background check. Thea's passport alerted me she has an ex. Has he threatened you personally, Gabi?"

She pressed her lips together. "No, but suffice it to say he was furious when Thea divorced him. If not for diplomatic immunity through Dad, I don't even want to think what might have happened to her. Dimitri considered her his possession. Thea was convinced he'd hired a man to follow her everywhere."

One black brow lifted sardonically. "My father and I have had business dealings with Dimitri's father in Athens. I'm familiar with his son's more devious methods."

That shouldn't have surprised Gabi. Andreas knew everything. "The trouble is, before she died she told me he was still out for blood wanting to know who made her pregnant. If he were to learn your brother is the father of her twins, he'd love to feed that kind of gossip to the newspapers just to be ugly."

"He can try," Andreas muttered with unconscious hauteur. After a palpable silence he said, "Since your parents must be waiting for you, I'll walk you back."

Gabi shook her head. "That won't be necessary."

"I insist."

He cupped her elbow and they started walking. Far too aware of his touch, she eased away from him as soon as they reached the street and moved ahead at a more brisk pace, but his long strides kept up with her.

When she nodded to the guard doing sentry duty, she thought of course Andreas would say goodnight. Instead he continued on through the front courtyard with her.

She halted. "You don't need to see me all the way to the front door."

"But I do. I want to speak to your parents."

What? Her body tautened in defense. "No,

Andreas! My parents aren't involved in this. That's the way I want it to stay. If Leon decides to claim the children, then I'll tell them everything. If there's any discussion about this, he's the one who needs to do it."

He cocked his head. "In an ideal world, it would work that way, but he's not ready yet."

That was obvious enough.

Reaching out, Andreas grasped her upper arms gently. She wished he wouldn't do that. It sent too many disturbing sensations through her body. Her awareness of him was overpowering.

"I have a plan that will solve our immediate problem, Gabi, but you're going to have to trust me."

Her eyes filled with tears. "Thea trusted me. Now look what's happening because I broke my promise to her. After her wretched divorce and subsequent death, my parents have suffered enough pain." Her voice throbbed. "Please just go." She stepped away from him.

His jaw hardened. "I can't, not when things haven't been resolved yet. You know the saying about being forewarned. If our two families know the truth and unite now, no power later on can shake our worlds. Don't you see?"

Yes. She could see there was no talking Andreas out of this. He wasn't the acting head of the Simonides Corporation for nothing. Gabi had only herself to blame. He'd asked her to trust him. Up until a minute ago she'd thought she could. But to go any further with this was like flying blind.

"I—I don't even know if they're still up." Her voice faltered.

"Then call them on your cell and alert them you've brought someone home with you."

She lowered her head. "I can't do that."

"Then I *will* because they deserve to know exactly what's going on."

A shiver raced through her body. Andreas had just put his finger on the thing tormenting her most. She'd hated doing all this behind her parents' backs. Defeated by his logic and her own guilt, she opened her purse and pulled out her phone. When she pushed the programmed digit, her mother answered on the second ring.

"Hi, darling? Where are you? I thought you'd be home before now."

She turned her back on Andreas. "When I went out, it was to meet a man I arranged to see in Athens the other day. He's with me now and wants to talk to you and Dad. I realize this sounds very cryptic."

The silence on the other end told its own story. "Do we know him?"

Gabi swallowed hard. "No, but you know *of* him by reputation." *You and everyone in Greece.*

"What's his name?"

"Andreas Simonides."

"Good heavens!" When the Simonides yacht was occasionally spotted outside Heraklion harbor, the whole city knew about it.

Gabi closed her eyes tightly for a second. "I realize it's getting late, but this is of vital importance. Prepare Dad, will you?"

"Of course. The babies are asleep. We'll be waiting for you in the salon."

"Thanks, Mom. You're one in a billion."

Andreas eyed her as she put the phone back in

her purse. "If you were looking for a job, I'd hire you as my personal assistant on your integrity and discretion alone."

She'd just received the supreme compliment from him, but the last thing she'd ever want to be was his personal secretary or anything else that put her in such close proximity to him for business reasons. No way would she allow herself to be put in emotional jeopardy like that again.

"Shall we go in?" She led the way to the front door and opened it. The salon was to the right of the main foyer where Gabi found her parents. Blonde and fit, she thought they were the most attractive people she knew. Andreas wouldn't be able to help but like their soft-spoken manner.

After she made the introductions, he sat forward in one of the chairs opposite the couch where they were seated. Gabi sat in another matching chair, knowing her parents were dying of curiosity.

"I've noticed you staring at me," Andreas began without preamble. "No doubt you've seen your grandsons' resemblance to me. That's because their father Leonides is my brother. We're identical twins, too. Twins run in the family."

While her parents digested that startling piece of information he said, "Nikos and Kris have an uncle Gus and two aunts, Melina and Leila. Until Gabi came to my office on Friday evening, my parents had ten grandchildren. But after our chat, I realized that number has grown to twelve."

"But this is unbelievable!" Gabi's mother exploded. She actually sounded relieved as she looked at Gabi's father. His burnished face had broken out in a smile, the last reaction Gabi would have imagined from either parent.

Andreas sent Gabi a satisfied glance. "Later, she'll fill you in on all the hows and whys of our first meeting. The important thing to know is that on Saturday, Leon met the children at the park.

"Unfortunately he's not ready to claim them yet. His wife Deline knows about his one-night relationship with your daughter Thea while he and Deline were separated. His pain and guilt over what he'd done drove him to go home the next day and talk everything out with her.

"It took a lot of gut-wrenching sessions and tears, but she eventually forgave him because she wasn't without her faults in the marriage, either. But that was a year ago and she has yet to learn he fathered two children. That's the hurdle facing him as we speak."

Gabi's parents squeezed hands.

"When Leon tells Deline about the twins, it could break up their marriage, possibly for good. The irony here is that they've been trying for a baby since the day they got married. It was one of the reasons they quarreled in the first place. She claimed he worked too hard and wasn't home long enough for them to start a family. So far they haven't been successful."

The added revelation hurt Gabi a little bit more. There'd been too much suffering all the way around.

"They'd been separated a while at the time he met Thea aboard the yacht. She'd come with a big group of friends, but Leon didn't know them. His friends had arranged it in order to party and cheer him up. His wife Deline had just told him she wanted a permanent separation. In his grief, he acted out unwisely. It doesn't excuse him for what he did, but it does explain his actions that night."

Gabi's father sat forward. "I'm afraid my daughter acted just as irresponsibly. Her marriage never took. When she won her divorce after a long battle, she made a wrong choice that night."

Andreas frowned, his brows black above his gray eyes. "Even if he was separated from his wife at the time, my brother's in a bad way because of his shame over making love to a virtual stranger when he was already married. His shame is even worse because he knows your daughter has passed away leaving two beautiful little babies who are his. Believe me, he's in anguish right now."

"He would be," her father murmured.

"Leon's my best friend, Mr. Turner. I know his heart."

Gabi bowed her head. She heard the love and

the caring in his tone. He really was a wonderful man.

"In another day or two when he's found the courage to tell his wife, he's going to want to see the children again and meet you. Hopefully at that point he'll be able to make some decisions in their best interest."

"I don't envy him," Gabi's mother murmured.

Neither did Gabi, but her thoughts were also on Andreas. This was no shallow man. The depth to his character kept hitting her harder and faster. Only a few days ago she'd thought he had ice water in his veins.

"I've come here tonight to urge Gabi not to go back to Virginia yet. I believe that if she stays in Greece another week where the children are accessible, something good will come of this.

"But she's told me her fears about Thea's ex-husband, Dimitri Paulos. I know him and his family through business. Apparently he became hostile when your daughter asked for a divorce. That's his way. Gabi's worried he's going to keep nosing around until he finds out who fathered

Thea's twins. She's afraid that if he learns it's Leon, he'll expose him to the press."

Her mother nodded. "He'd do it without a qualm."

By now Gabi's father had gotten to his feet. "I'm afraid he turned on me when I helped my daughter obtain her divorce."

"It happens. But by the time my brother comes to grips with this situation one way or the other, it will have lost its sensational value. For now I'd like to suggest Gabi and the children be removed to an undisclosed place that's still close enough for Leon to have immediate access."

Gabi blinked. "Where?"

Andreas shot her a penetrating look. "I know the perfect spot," he said with authority and got to his feet. "It's late. Walk me out and we'll talk about it."

The next few minutes were a blur while her parents thanked him for his frank speaking and dealing with this delicate situation head-on. Before he joined her at the front door, there'd been hugs to welcome the twins' uncle to the family. The man was endowed with charm from the gods.

She went outside with him. The balmy night air seemed to make the moment more intimate somehow. Strange little tingles brought an ache to her hands. When she looked up at him, she felt her body come to life with feelings she'd thought Rand had killed. But it wasn't true.

This couldn't be happening again. It just couldn't!

In the semi-darkness she felt his piercing gaze travel over her features. "Gabi?" he said her name in his deep voice. "Will you continue to trust me for a little while longer?"

It was hard to swallow. "After approaching you first, I'm hardly in a position to refuse now. Do your parents know anything yet?"

"No. Leon wants to tell them when he's ready."

"So you have to continue to be the keeper of all the secrets."

"I don't mind."

No, because she was learning what kind of

a man he really was. "You have a lot on your shoulders."

"So do you. In fact you've inherited the bulk by taking care of the twins. I'd like to help you with that. We'll think of it as a vacation time for both of us. After all, they're part my flesh and blood."

"Andreas? Are you married, too?" Before she took another breath she needed the answer to that question. "I haven't seen a wedding ring, but I realize some men don't wear them."

In the silence that followed, she felt his sudden tension. "I'm still single. You don't need to be worried I'm keeping secrets from a wife or neglecting her for Leon's sake."

Single. His answer frightened her because she no longer trusted herself around him. When she'd promised to never let a man get under her skin again, Andreas had already found entrance, slipping past her guard totally undetected.

"W-where is this safe place?" she stammered.

"On Milos, in a little village called Apollonia. I realize you're leaving in the morning, but I hope you'll give my idea serious thought. Either way I'll expect a call from you later tonight. Sleep well, *despinis*."

CHAPTER FOUR

ANDREAS had two phone calls to make. The first was one he'd known was coming ever since Gabi had entered his office, or rather blown in with that head of curly golden hair and eyes like the periwinkle bougainvillea outside his villa door.

Like the Venus de Milo unearthed in the ancient town of Milos where he used to dig around the ruins as a boy, Gabi's feminine shape appealed to his senses. With his six-foot-three height, he'd never been partial to shorter women or blondes until now, a fact that surprised the daylights out of him.

Her guileless honesty combined with her intensity had intrigued him. If he were to admit to all the traits he'd found fascinating and endearing since watching her with the twins, the list would be endless.

Something earthshaking had happened to him. Already he felt a changed man. Right or wrong, his desire to be with Gabi was so profound, he realized he had to break it off with Irena.

To feel this way about another woman wasn't fair to her. He hadn't planned for this to happen. It just did…

Maybe Andreas's feelings for Gabi would die a quick death, but until that eventuality he *had* to explore them because he'd never known this kind of excitement over a woman in his life. Somewhere in his gut he knew these feelings weren't all on his side. Gabi wouldn't have asked him if he was married if her emotions weren't involved, too.

Tonight, when they were outside the consulate, it was all he could do not to pull her in his arms and kiss them both into oblivion.

After his shower he hitched a towel around his hips and reached for his cell. It rang until Irena's voice mail came on. Frustrated because this wasn't something he wanted to do by phone anyway, he started to click off when he heard her speak.

"Andreas—don't hang up. I was in the other room and had almost given up on hearing from you tonight. I've missed you."

Guilt smote him. The last time they'd talked had been Friday. Now it was Tuesday night. In that short amount of time he hadn't missed her at all. Another woman had filled his thoughts to the exclusion of everything else. How could that be?

"Irena? Forgive me."

"You know I do."

Yes, he knew.

"Something's definitely wrong. You sound so different."

Heaven knew his world had changed. "I'm not sure how to say this except to come straight to the point because you deserve my total honesty. Up until last Friday you've been the only woman in my life."

A long pause ensued. "And now you're telling me there's someone else?"

He bowed his head. "Let's just say I met some-one." Andreas couldn't believe he'd admitted it to the woman he'd loved and had been planning to ask to marry him. It meant Gabi had a hold on him more profound than even he had realized. "I swear this was the last thing I ever expected to be saying to you."

More silence. "Does she feel the same way?" Irena finally asked in a subdued voice. There were never any tantrums with her. She wasn't like that. He wished she would rage at him. Instead there was this condemning quiet that underlined her pain.

"I sense she's not indifferent to me, but I haven't acted on my feelings yet."

"But you *want* to?"

He drew in a ragged breath. "I would never hurt you purposely, Irena, but until I explore what's going on inside of me, being with you right now wouldn't be fair to you. That's why I'm calling."

More silence. "Won't you at least come to the house so we can talk about this?"

"I will when I'm back in Athens."

"Where are you?"

His hand tightened on the receiver. "I'm on Crete and can't leave." He was in a hotel, wondering how he would be able to wait until morning when he saw Gabi again.

"Does she know about us?"

There's no us. Not anymore. "No."

"Who is she?"

Irena deserved that much. "An American who came to my office because of a life and death situation. She had business with me no one else could help her with. I'm still helping her solve a very serious problem before she returns to the States."

"I see," she whispered.

Except she didn't see. How could she? Andreas wanted to tell her everything, but he couldn't until he knew what Leon was going to do. Irena was best friends with Deline. The whole situation was more complicated than anyone knew.

He clutched the phone tighter. "I know I've hurt you, Irena, but to be less than honest with you at this point would be unconscionable."

"Your father told me your courage is one of your most remarkable traits. After this conversation I have to say I agree with him. I love you, Andreas. I know you did love me in your own way. But you were never *in* love with me, otherwise—" She broke off talking. He knew what she was going to say, that otherwise they would have married months ago. "I'm going to hang up now." The line went dead.

Horrible as he felt for hurting her, relief swept through him that from here on out he wouldn't be lying to her or Gabi.

Before he let any more time pass, he had a second call to make to Leon, who was vacationing for the next two weeks on Milos with Deline and the rest of the family. With Gabi sequestered in Apollonia on the north end of the island nine kilometers from the Simonides villa, the timing and proximity couldn't be better.

In anticipation of her falling in with his plan, he'd made all the arrangements ahead of time. Now there was nothing left to do but inform his brother, who'd known this call was coming.

As soon as they spoke he'd never heard Leon sound so upset. He hadn't told Deline the truth yet, but knew he had to.

After encouraging him not to wait any longer, Andreas hung up to wait for Gabi's phone call. If she chose to fly back to the States in the morning, then he'd take her and the twins home in the company jet.

Gabi's father patted the side of the bed and stared at her with solemn eyes. "When did Thea tell you about Leon Simonides?"

With that question she realized it was going to be a long night. She sat down next to him. "Right before she died." After clearing her throat she said, "All along Thea thought the man she'd made love with was Andreas. That's why I went to his office."

Her parents listened intently as she explained what had happened to Thea. "When she swore me to secrecy, I intended to honor my promise to her. But after she died, I kept looking at the babies and thinking how terrible it would be if they never knew their father, either. I realized I couldn't go through life with that kind of a secret."

"Of course you couldn't." Her father pulled her into his arms. "I love you more than ever for what you've done."

"So do I," her mother cried. "It took tremendous courage, darling."

"I'm sorry to have lied about my reason for going to Athens on Friday, but I didn't know if I'd be able to get in to see Andreas."

"Thank heaven you did. Honestly, when he walked in the salon, it was like looking at the children all grown up."

Her dad shook his head. "I'm still amazed by what we've learned. He's a very remarkable man. A good one. No wonder he's at the head of the Simonides empire."

"You should see him with the boys, Dad. The way he responds, you'd think *he* was their father." Her voice shook.

Her mother reached over to press her arm. "What's Leon like?"

"I can't tell yet. He was in shock on Saturday and hardly spoke, but the fact that he came at all speaks of his character." She wiped her eyes.

"Seeing those two brothers together will really be something," her mom said. "That's how it's going to be for Kris and Nikos."

Gabi nodded. "Thea was so beautiful, and

they're so handsome already. When they've become men, they'll be as spectacular as Andreas—I mean Leon."

"Does he know Kris will have to undergo a series of surgeries in the future?"

"Not yet, Mom," she mumbled.

"Why didn't you tell him?"

"Because I knew Leon was in shock. When I put myself in his place, I realized how hard it would be for him to tell his wife. I suppose I didn't want to scare him off or have him thinking I was after his money to pay for the medical expenses."

Gabi's father patted her arm. "Tell Andreas. He'll know the best way to broach his brother."

Her dad was right. "I will."

"Do his parents know anything yet?"

"No."

"So where is this safe place he was talking about?"

She slid off the bed, too filled with nervous energy to sit any longer. "On Milos."

"Of course," her father said. "Their family

compound is on that island in a private bay that is better guarded than the White House."

"Actually, he mentioned I'd be staying at a nearby village called Apollonia, but I don't know any of the details yet. He said to leave everything to him, but I have to be sure it's the right thing to do. I told him I would have to think about it. He's waiting for a phone call from me tonight."

Her dad cleared his throat. "I guess your mother and I don't have to tell you how wonderful it would be to know you and the children are close by while Leon is deciding what to do. Naturally I'd prefer that you stayed right here and—"

"No, Dad," she interrupted him. "I don't know how you've done your work through all this, but it's time you were able to concentrate on the job you were appointed to. You have too many dignitaries coming and going to put up with so much distraction."

"You and the children are hardly a distraction, Gabi."

"You know what I mean. Your life isn't

conventional. You need to get back to it. Andreas told me to think of this as a vacation."

Her mother flicked her a thoughtful glance. "If Leon realizes he wants his children, then you have to admit Andreas has come up with a temporary solution that suits everyone. A week from now and everything could be settled. But it's your decision."

That was what was haunting Gabi. No decision sounded like the right one.

If Leon wanted to claim his children and raise them, then she would be free to get back to her old life in the States. But her world had changed so dramatically since her arrival on Crete four months ago, she didn't know herself anymore.

The twins had come to mean everything to her. As for Andreas… She kneaded her hands. He was waiting for her to get back to him.

She paused in the doorway fighting conflicting emotions. "Andreas is doing everything in his power to unite his brother with his own babies. I started all this and need to finish it, so I'll tell him yes. See you in the morning."

Once out the door she rushed down the hall to her room to make the phone call. He answered on the second ring.

"Gabi?" came the deep voice she could pick out over anyone's. "Did you discuss this with your family?"

"Yes." She struggled to sound calm. "The children need their father. If my coming to Milos will hasten the process, then so be it."

"Good. Now here's what I want you to do. Follow through exactly with the plans you and your parents have for tomorrow morning. But when you arrive at the airport, tell the driver to take you through to the heliport where my helicopter will be waiting. I'll be there to help you and the boys aboard."

"All right." She gripped the phone tighter. "Andreas—there's something else you need to know. I should have told you before now, but I was afraid."

"Of what?"

"That you would believe what you first thought about me—that I was out to get money from you."

"Go on."

"This concerns Kris."

"What about him?" Just now she heard a raw edge to his voice.

"He was born with a defective aortic valve in his heart. No one knows why. He didn't inherit anything genetic from Thea. She didn't develop heart trouble until she became pregnant. His condition is called stenosis."

"I noticed he's a little smaller."

Most people saw no difference in the twins, but nothing got past Andreas. "According to his pediatrician here in Heraklion, he'll have to undergo his first operation next month. I'd planned to have the surgery done in Alexandria with a highly recommended pediatric heart specialist."

"We have one of the best here in Athens," Andreas murmured, sounding far away. "How many procedures will be required?"

"Maybe only one more after that. The doctor said most valves have to be replaced every two to three years, but with non-embryonic stem-cell heart tissue, the replacement valve should grow as Kris grows and no more surgery will be necessary. That's what we're hoping and praying for."

"Amen to that."

She put a hand to her throat. "When do you think you'll tell your brother?"

"Tonight. He needs to be apprised of all the facts before you're settled on Milos. In the next few weeks he and I will start giving blood for Kris's fund."

"Our family plans to give some, too. To look at him you wouldn't know anything's wrong. He's so precious."

"Until now I've never coveted anything of my brother's."

"I know what you mean. If the gods were giving out perfect children, you wouldn't have to look any further than Kris and Nikos."

"No," came the husky rejoinder. "Get a good sleep for what's left of the rest of the night, Gabi. Tomorrow's a new day for all of us."

"Andreas—"

"Yes?"

"I just wanted to say that I think Leon is very

lucky to have a brother like you. Would that the twins develop that kind of love for each other. Goodnight."

"We're coming up on the little fishing village of Apollonia, named after the god Apollo." Andreas had been giving Gabi an insider's tour of the Cyclades from his position in the co-pilot's seat.

She'd never been to Milos. As the pilot swung the helicopter toward the beautiful island sparkling like a gem in the blue Aegean Gabi's breath caught. She'd once visited the islands of Mykonos and Kea on the ferry, not by air. To see all the fantastic volcanic formations and colorful beaches from this height robbed her of words.

During the flight from Heraklion, her awe-struck gaze had met his many times. Maybe it was a trick of light from being at this altitude in a cloudless sky, but when he looked at her the gray of his irises seemed to turn crystalline, almost like a glowing silver fire.

The twins were strapped down in their carry-cots opposite her so she could watch them.

They'd stayed awake during the flight, good as gold.

"Is that Apollonia down there hugging the bay?" she questioned as they drew closer.

Andreas chuckled. "No. That's the home of the Simonides clan. Apollonia is just beyond it."

Gabi was staggered. She stared at the twins. Little did they know the lineage they came from included a kingdom as magical as anything she'd seen in a fairy tale. But instead of towers and turrets and drawbridges, it was a gleaming white cluster of cubical beauty set against an impossibly turquoise-blue sea found only in this part of the world.

Further on lay the picturesque little town where she'd be staying. It was built in the typical royal blue and white motif along a sandy beach, the kind you saw in videos and on postcards advertising the charm of the Greek islands. Before the helicopter landed, she knew she was going to love it here.

She picked out the boats at the village pier. There appeared to be myriad shops and restaurants close by, an idyllic vacation spot if there ever was one. As soon as they landed and the blades stopped rotating, Andreas helped her and the twins into a car waiting by the helipad.

The pilot loaded her luggage and the stroller into the trunk. There was a considerable amount of stuff. She poked her head out the window. "Thank you!" she called to him. "When you travel with babies, there's no such thing as packing light."

Both men flashed each other a grin before Andreas took his place behind the wheel and started the motor. Seated across from his hardmuscled body, Gabi felt an excitement out of all proportion to the reason why she and the twins had been whisked to this heavenly place.

He drove them past tavernas and bars, pointing out a supermarket and a bakery where she could buy anything she needed. In a few minutes they turned onto a private road that wound beneath a cluster of trees and ended at a perfectly charming blue and white house with its own shaded garden and stone walkways.

Gabi let out a sound of pleasure. "This is an adorable place, Andreas."

"I'm glad you like it. From the front door you step right out onto the beach. The house is fully air-conditioned, another reason why I chose it."

"The babies and I will be happy as clams here."

He darted her a curious look. "That's an odd American expression. Do you think clams are happy?"

She burst into laughter. "I have no idea, but I know we will be."

His low chuckle followed her as she got out of the car to open the back door. By now the twins were so awake they were eager to escape their confinement. While she released Kris's carry-cot from the strap, Andreas removed Nikos. Together they walked toward the door where a pretty, dark-haired woman who looked to be in her mid-twenties held it open for them.

"*Kalimera*, Kyrie Simonides."

"*Kalimera*, Lena. This is Gabi Turner." The two women smiled. "Lena and her husband manage this resort. They have a son, Basil, who's five months old."

"Oh—I'd love to see him."

"He's with my husband right now, but I'll bring him out to the garden later in the day. How old are your children?"

"Three months."

"They are very beautiful." Lena's glance slid to Andreas, no doubt trying to figure out their relationship when the wiggling babies looked like *him*, not Gabi. "We have maid service. If you need anything, pick up the phone and the office will answer."

"Thank you. This is delightful."

"I think so, too. Enjoy your stay."

After she walked off, they moved through to the living room whose white interior was accented with dark wood furniture and blue accessories. "What a charming house!" she cried.

"I'm glad you like it." Andreas sounded pleased as she followed him through to one of the bedrooms down the hall where two cribs and a set of dresser drawers had been set up. Everything was impeccably clean.

Andreas helped her lift the boys out of their carry-cots and lay them down in their cribs. "I'll bring in your things."

"That would be wonderful." She kissed Kris. "The babies have been awake for a long time and are getting impatient for their lunch, but first they're going to need a diaper change."

"Afterward I'll help you feed them."

"That won't be necessary."

"What if I want to?"

His playful teasing didn't fool her. "You've done more than enough, Andreas. I can just picture your exceptional receptionist wondering where on earth you've disappeared to."

She watched him kiss Nikos. "Didn't I tell you I'm on vacation? The whole family's here for the next two weeks."

This time her heart really did get a major workout. "As I recall, you were going to give me an appointment at three o'clock yesterday afternoon."

"If *you* recall," he murmured, coming to stand next to her, bringing his warmth and enticing male scent with him, "a life and death situation altered the scheme of our lives."

Gabi gripped the railing of the crib tighter. *Our* lives was right. When she'd gone to his office in Athens on Friday, the idea that days later she'd be alone with him on Milos would have stretched the limits of her imagination. Yet here she was…

"For the time being, my first priority is to lend Leon moral support." On that succinct note he left the bedroom.

While he was gone she gave herself another lecture about remembering why she'd been temporarily ensconced in this corner of paradise. Leon was blessed to have his brother's backing. As Gabi's father had said, Andreas was a good man. *How* good no one would ever know who hadn't walked in her footsteps since last Friday evening when she'd first confronted him.

In a few minutes he'd returned with the diaper bag and bottles of formula already prepared. They changed the babies before going into the living room to feed them. He was as confident and efficient as any seasoned father. Whether

Leon ended up raising them or not, Andreas had claimed his nephews. She had an idea he would be an intrinsic part of their lives from now on.

After they put the twins down for their nap, Andreas announced he was leaving for his villa. "I'll be back with food before they're awake." He flicked her a heavy-lidded glance before disappearing from the house.

While she was taking clothes out of the suitcase to hang up and put in drawers, she heard the car drive off. He'd told her the Simonides compound was only ten minutes away by car, but already she missed him. To keep herself busy she acquainted herself with the rest of the house.

A perfect little kitchen containing snacks and a fridge stocked with drinks connected to the living room. On the other side was a hall with a bathroom separating two bedrooms. Hers had a shady terrace with loungers and a table looking out on the translucent water. The pots of flowers and an overhang of fuchsia-colored bougainvillea on the trellis gave off a subtle perfume.

Gabi hugged her arms to her waist, hardly

able to contain the rush of euphoria that swept through her. She was in that dangerous state where the lines were blurred and she was imagining something quite different than the reality of her situation.

The beach was calling to her, so, with Lena's assurance that she would watch over the babies, Gabi changed into her two-piece aqua-colored swimming suit. A month ago she'd wandered into a little shop in Heraklion and had bought the most modestly cut outfit she could find, but it still revealed more than she liked. A tan might have helped, but this hadn't been a summer to relax in the sun.

After smoothing on some sunscreen, she grabbed a large striped towel and left for the beach through the terrace exit. A person could step down to the sand where the sea was only ten yards away, no more. It shimmered like a rare aquamarine. She dropped the towel and ran out, luxuriating in the calm water whose temperature had to be in the seventies.

Gabi swam for a while, then floated around on her back while she watched various sailboats and the occasional ferry in the distance. There were a few other people farther down the beach, but for the most part she had this area to herself. Doing a somersault, she swam underwater to examine the shallow sea floor before surfacing to reach the beach and stretch out on her towel.

While she lay there on her stomach thinking this was pure heaven, she heard a motor that signaled a boat was approaching. When the sound was suddenly cut, she lifted her head from her arms and realized a ski boat had glided right up on the sand.

Her double vision was back as two Greek gods in dark swimming trunks jumped down from the sides with the kind of agility any male would kill for and walked in her direction.

"Andreas—" She sat up with a start, taking the towel with her to give herself a little protection from his all-seeing eyes. Then she remembered her manners, her gaze darting to his brother. "How are you, Leon?"

A faint smile hovered around his lips. "More in control than I was a few nights ago. I apologize for my rude behavior."

She shook her head. "There's no need."

"There's *every* need," he insisted, reminding her of a forceful Andreas. "I should be the one asking you how you are. You've been taking care of my sons all this time and I never knew."

Gabi smiled. "They're my nephews so it's no sacrifice, believe me."

"May I go in and see them?" He was making the effort, she'd give him that.

"Of course. If they start to fuss, there are bottles of formula made up in the fridge. Just warm them up in some hot water. Andreas?" She flicked her gaze back to him. "Why don't you show him their room while I go for another swim? If they wake up, it will be lovely for them to see their daddy."

His white smile had a domino effect that slowly melted every bone in her body. "When you surface again, climb up the back ladder into the boat and I'll take you for a ride. While Leon gets acquainted with them, we'll enjoy a picnic on the water."

"That sounds good. I'm getting hungry." It

was already three-thirty. She'd lost track of the time.

"So am I." His husky tone caused a ripple effect through her body.

The second they disappeared through the front door, she hurried into the bedroom via the terrace and grabbed a loose-fitting short sundress with spaghetti straps she often wore over her suit as a cover-up.

Their deep male voices faded as she rushed back to the beach. After shaking out the towel, she walked in the water and chucked her things in the back of the boat before climbing in. By the time Andreas emerged from the house, she was presentable enough to feel comfortable being with him.

He ran toward her, shoving the boat back into the water, then he levered himself effortlessly over the side. His brief glance managed to take in all of her before he started the motor. "We'll head for Kimolos." He nodded toward an island that couldn't be more than a mile away. "The sight of the little village of Psathi is worth the short trip."

Halfway across, he turned off the engine and joined her in the back so they could eat. In the hamper were sodas, fruit and homemade gyros. No food had ever tasted so good. She didn't have to search for a reason why.

"Thank you for a wonderful meal. In fact this whole trip."

Andreas stared at her while he munched on an apple. "Thank *you* for not giving up trying to get in to see me."

Gabi knew what he meant. Her mouth curved in a half-smile. "We need to thank your receptionist. Without her going out on a limb for me, that would have been the end of it." Then a slight frown marred her brow. "But maybe it would have been better if she hadn't had compassion on me."

Lines darkened his striking features. "Don't *ever* say that. I don't even want to think about it."

Neither did she. A world without Andreas was incomprehensible to her. She finished her cola. "What are your brother's feelings by now?"

Letting out a heavy sigh, he closed his eyes

and lay back on the padded bench to get the full effect of the sun for a moment. End to end, his toned physique with its smattering of dark hair plus his chiseled profile proved to be too much for her. She turned her head to stare anywhere but at him.

"If the twins hadn't tugged at Leon's heart the first time he saw them, he wouldn't have agreed to my plan for you to bring them here. When I told him Kris has to go in for heart surgery next month, that seemed to jar him to the reality of the situation. But he's terrified because he loves Deline and is afraid he'll lose her when she learns the truth."

"I can't imagine being in his position."

After a silence, "If you were Deline, do you think *you* could handle it?"

His searching question brought her head around. They looked at each other for a long time. "I don't honestly know. She forgave him for what happened a year ago, but now that the other woman's children are involved…"

She bowed her head. "If I loved him desperately, it might be possible. At the time he didn't know he'd gotten my sister pregnant, but I'm not Deline. Do they have the kind of love for each other to deal with it?"

He jackknifed into a sitting position and put his feet on the floor of the boat. His eyes looked haunted. "After he tells her, I guess they're going to find out how solid their marriage really is."

Gabi stirred restlessly. "He needs to do it soon. Every day that passes while he keeps it from her will make it harder for her to trust him."

"I told him that the night he saw the children at the park."

"Andreas—much as I'd love to go sightseeing with you this afternoon to give him more time with the twins, I think we should go back. You need to impress on him that if he waits even another day, it might be too late to convince Deline of anything."

"I agree," his voice rasped.

"Trust is everything. If Leon wants to prove his love, then he needs to approach her *now*."

He nodded. "Not only that, every day he's away from his sons, he's losing that vital bonding time with them." Andreas sprang to his feet. "Let's go."

With the sea so placid, they made it back to the beach in a flash, but Gabi had returned in a completely different frame of mind than when they'd headed for open water. She jumped into the shallows carrying her towel above her head and walked in the front door of the house ahead of Andreas.

To her surprise, Leon had brought the children into the living room. It was a touching scene to see the three of them spread out on the quilt together. Nikos lay next to his daddy, who held Kris in the air, kissing his tummy to produce smiles.

Andreas's eyes looked suspiciously bright as he darted her a glance that spoke volumes. While she held back, not wanting to interrupt, he lifted Nikos from the floor and cuddled him.

Leon stood up with Kris pressed against his shoulder. "I can't believe they're mine." He spoke into the baby's soft black hair. He was totally natural with the children now.

"I dare say you've produced the most beautiful sons in the entire Simonides clan."

He eyed Andreas with a soulful look. "No matter what, I have to tell Deline today. Come with me, bro."

What Gabi had been hoping for had come to pass, yet with those words *no matter what* she felt a door close on her secret dream of adopting the twins herself. It was as if her heart had just been cut out of her body.

CHAPTER FIVE

"Gabi?" Leon had turned to her. "I'm not sure when I'll be back. Do you mind being responsible for the twins a while longer? You know what I mean."

Yes. She knew exactly, but by some miracle she didn't give in to the impulse to break into hysterical sobbing. "I've loved taking care of my nephews and want to help you any way I can. Why don't you put the children back in their cribs so I can change them?" she suggested in the brightest voice she could muster.

As they headed for the bedroom she was aware of Andreas's avid gaze leveled on her, but she managed to avoid contact. He could see inside her soul. If she were to make the mistake of looking at him, her composure would dissolve. This was a pivotal moment for Leon. An emotional meltdown on her part now could ruin everything.

Thankful after they'd left the room and she could hear the rev of the boat engine, Gabi put clean diapers on the twins and got them ready for an evening walk around the village in their stroller. Next to the bakery was a deli where she could buy some food ready to go.

Once she'd showered and had dressed in a matching blue skirt and sleeveless top, she wheeled them out of the back door. Lena happened to be pushing her little boy along in his stroller as she did some weeding.

The two of them talked and pretty soon they went into the village together. Gabi enjoyed the other woman's company. It helped not to think about the loss that was coming. If she were honest, it wasn't only the twins she was already missing…

Three hours later she was putting the babies to bed when her cell rang. The sight of Andreas's name on the caller ID caused a fluttery sensation in her chest.

"Hello?" She knew she sounded anxious.

"I called as soon as I could, Gabi."

"You don't owe me anything. H-has Leon told his wife?" Her voice faltered.

"Yes."

His silence made her clutch the phone tighter. "Was it awful?"

"I won't lie to you. It was a great deal worse."

Tears clogged her throat. "I'm so sorry."

"So am I. She's threatened to divorce him and has flown back to Athens in the helicopter. I just drove him to the island's airport so he could take a plane to catch up to her."

A whole new world of pain had opened up for them.

When Thea had divorced Dimitri, Gabi had been overjoyed, but this was an entirely different situation. From all accounts Deline was a lovely woman who didn't deserve to have any of this happen to her. Neither did the babies. But the fact remained Leon and Thea had made a mistake that had caused heartbreak in every direction.

"Does your family know the reason they left Milos?"

"Not yet, but it's only a matter of time," he ground out.

She moistened her lips nervously. "What would your brother like me to do?"

"Stay right where you are. I'll bring the car around at eight-thirty in the morning. We'll drive to the pier where the cabin cruiser will be waiting. I need a solid break and intend to show you the sights of the island. Pack enough formula in case we want to dock somewhere overnight. Stavros will take care of everything else."

Her body trembled.

An invitation to party overnight on the Simonides yacht had proved too much of a temptation for Thea. Gabi wasn't any different. The desire to spend uninterrupted time with the twins' uncle aboard his cabin cruiser filled her with secret longings that had her jumping out of her skin.

When she thought about it, she would never again have the opportunity to be with a man who thrilled her the way Andreas did. In a few days Leon would make definitive plans where the twins were concerned and Gabi would be leaving Greece.

So why not enjoy this time with Andreas? As long as she recognized he was a bachelor who didn't take his relationships with women seriously, then she wouldn't either. She'd learned her lesson with Rand.

In the future she would come to visit her family and the twins from time to time, but she had a career waiting for her back in Virginia. The boys' lives were here with their father. They would need to get used to the nanny Leon would employ to help him.

Gabi couldn't possibly stay around, otherwise none of it would work; therefore this little bit of time on Apollonia was all she was going to get with Andreas. As she'd told his receptionist on Friday, "I'll take it!"

"Eight-thirty's a perfect time. The three of us will be ready. Goodnight, Andreas." She hung up before she betrayed herself and kept him on the phone if only to listen to the sound of his deep, mellifluous voice.

* * *

With the babies down until their next feeding, Andreas instructed Stavros to bring the cruiser as close to the cave opening as possible. A side glance revealed that a golden-haired nymph had come to join him on the swim platform and was ready to dive with him.

Her modest two-piece suit only seemed to add to the allure of her beautifully proportioned body. Compared to the bronzed females he'd seen at various beaches throughout the day wearing little or nothing at all, her delicious femininity and creamy skin—unused to so much sun—drew his gaze over and over again.

"Are you sure you want to try this, Gabi? We've done a lot of swimming today. If you're tired, we can explore here in the morning."

She flashed him a mischievous smile that gave his heart a wallop of a kick. "After the big buildup about an evening swim at your favorite beach, you couldn't stop me!"

Without warning she leaped off the side and headed through the cave opening to Papafragas beach at a very credible speed.

Andreas hadn't had this much fun in years and followed her into the cool water. Beyond the opening was a long, natural, fjordlike swimming pool surrounded by walls of white rock. He heard her cry of delight.

"This is fabulous, Andreas!" Her voice created an echo.

He caught up to her and they both treaded water. "You can see the deep caves where pirates used to hide."

Her lips twitched. "Even modern-day pirates like the Simonides twins, I would wager." She kept turning around, looking up at the incredible rock formations. "It's time for the truth, Andreas. Between you and Leon, how many girls did you used to bring here on an evening like this, pretending surprise that you were the only ones about?"

His laughter created another echo. "You've caught me out. We brought our share. It's true that this late in the day most tourists have gone back to wherever they came from." He'd planned it this way because he'd wanted Gabi to himself.

"Come on. I'll race you to the beach at the other end."

Another fifty yards lay a strip of sand still warm from the sun, though its rays no longer penetrated here. She reached it first and sank down in it, turning over so she could look up at the sky. "Oh-h-h, this feels so good I'll never want to move again."

"Then we won't." Andreas stretched out on his stomach next to her. He couldn't remember the last time he'd felt this alive.

A come-hither smile broke one corner of her delectable mouth. "We'll have to, if only for the twins' sake."

"They're being watched over. For the moment I'd like to forget everything and everyone and simply concentrate on you." He raised up on one elbow. "You know what I want to do to you."

The little pulse at her throat was throbbing madly. "Yes," she whispered in an aching voice.

A moan sounded deep in his throat. That was all he was waiting to hear before leaning down to lower his mouth to hers. He needed her kiss as much as he needed air to breathe. At the first taste of her, he was shaken by her breathtaking response. After coaxing her lips apart he began drinking deeply. Back and forth they gave each other one hungry kiss after another until it all became a blend of needs they fought to assuage.

Heedless of the fine sand covering their bodies, he rolled her on top of him, craving the perfect fit of her in his arms, the sweet scent of her. "You're so beautiful, Gabi," he murmured against the side of her tender neck. "Do you have any idea how much I want you?"

"Andreas—" The tremor in her voice told him she was equally caught up in the surge of passion sweeping them into a world where nothing existed but their desire for each other.

"What is it?" he whispered after wresting another kiss from her incredible mouth.

"I feel out of control," she admitted against his lips.

He molded her body to his with more urgency. "That's the way you're supposed to feel when it's right. I can't get enough of you." So saying, he kissed her again until they were both devouring each other.

Never having known rapture like this, he wasn't prepared when she suddenly tore her lips away and rolled off him. "Where did you go?" he cried before sitting up. "We're not in any hurry."

"Maybe not, but I'm out of breath and need to slow down before we start back."

He kissed her shoulder. "If you're too tired when we're ready to go, I'll help you."

"You mean you'll get me out of here using the old reliable life-saving technique? Just how far do you think we'd get?" Gabi teased. She'd turned her head, focusing her dark-fringed eyes on him. Their color changed with the surroundings. Right now they'd picked up some of the gray-blue of the water.

"In my condition and the way I'm feeling at the moment, not far, but in time I'd manage it."

"I believe you would," she said with a smile that was too bright after what they'd just shared. His eyes narrowed on the erotic flare of her mouth, an enticement that lured him like Desponia's song. She could pretend all she wanted, but in each other's arms they'd both been shaken by a force that was only going to grow in strength.

"Sometimes I think you're half god the way you make things happen. It's like magic."

"Would that I had the magic to put my brother's world back together."

"I could wish for the same thing."

She got up from the sand and walked into the water to wash off. Bringing her to this spot had been in the back of his mind since last night. He couldn't bear it that they were forced to leave, but they had to get back to the twins.

Although he'd allowed Gabi to believe otherwise, he'd never brought another woman here before, not even Irena. She liked an occasional dip in a swimming pool, but she wasn't adventurous, not like Gabi, who'd sprung onto the canvas of his life with an unexpectedness that had left him reeling.

Until today he could have told Irena that everything he'd done to help his brother through a nightmarish, unprecedented situation had been necessary and it would have been the truth. But being out here with Gabi would have been impossible to explain. More than ever he was thankful he'd broken it off with her.

She would have pointed out that the twins' aunt was already staying in a vacation spot that provided every possible distraction without requiring Andreas's assistance. He would have had no excuse for spending the rest of today and tonight with her on his cabin cruiser. No excuse for coming close to making love to her.

While she treaded water, he threw his head back and looked up at the darkening sky, wishing this night never had to end.

"We'd better go, Gabi." The words came out harsh, even to his own ears. "Do you think you're up to it?"

"I was afraid maybe you weren't and I would have to save *you*," she quipped. So saying, she took off like a golden sea sprite, leaving behind a trail of tinkling laughter he found utterly irresistible.

* * *

Gabi gripped the rings that helped her climb the ladder into the boat. After rinsing off in the shower of the swim platform, she wrapped up in a towel and moved toward the rear cockpit where Andreas was talking to Stavros.

She smiled at him. "Did you think we were never coming back and you'd have to deal with two howling babies wanting their feeding in the middle of the night?"

The older man's eyes twinkled. "We would have managed."

"Have they been good?"

"Like little angels."

"I'm glad, then." She raised up on tiptoe to kiss his cheek. "Thank you for being a wonderful babysitter."

Gabi was still trying to catch her breath, as much from the physical exertion of attempting to outdistance Andreas—which was an impossibility—as having been alone with him.

There'd been a moment on the sand when she'd wanted to know his possession so badly, she'd almost expired on the spot. But she knew better than to repeat the mistakes of the past.

She had no doubt Andreas wanted her. He'd been forthcoming about it, and the desire between them had been building until she was ready to burst. Those kisses on the beach were inevitable, but she was wise enough not to read anything more into them. That was why she'd swum for her life back there, so she wouldn't forget the promise she'd made to herself to focus all her energy on her career.

She flicked her host a steady glance. "When I'm back at my job inundated with work, I'll remember this glorious day. Thank you."

"There's more to see tomorrow before we get back to Apollonia," Andreas reminded her.

Gabi knew what that meant. Her pulse throbbed without her permission. "I'm looking forward to it," she said bravely. "Goodnight."

Not daring to meet his eyes this time, she darted down the steps to her cabin off the passageway. Relieved the children lay sound asleep in their carry-cots, she quickly showered again and washed her hair before climbing into bed.

Since spending time on the boat, she'd learned that his stateroom was on the other side of the wall. One more thing she'd picked up from Stavros. This cabin cruiser was Andreas's home when he really wanted to get away on his own.

Gabi realized the older man had let her know she was a privileged person, but she could tell him that without the babies she would never have been given entrée to Andreas's private world.

Almost a week ago today she'd gone to his office. Since then she'd spent some time with him, yet she still didn't know anything about his personal life. He'd only volunteered information on a need-to-know basis. Love for his brother was the sole reason she'd been invited aboard this boat.

With time on his hands, he'd done the natural thing and had kissed her because he knew the attraction was mutual. The same thing had happened with Rand. She'd been a guest on his ranch and he'd enjoyed her to the fullest *as long as she was there*.

Those were the key words to help her keep her head on straight with Andreas until she went back to Alexandria.

Three o'clock was going to be here before she knew it. With the memory of him lying next to her on that sandy beach where she could still feel the taste of his mouth on hers, she closed her eyes, fearing she'd never be able to sleep. But to her shock the twins didn't start crying until seven-thirty the next morning.

Maybe it was the sea air or the gentle sway of the boat. Whatever, they'd actually slept through the night!

After she'd bathed and fed them, she got dressed in shorts and a top before carrying them up on deck one at a time. Already the sun was warm. Stavros had breakfast waiting for her on the up-and-down table, another remarkable invention aboard the cruiser.

"Mmm, that looks delicious. Good morning, Stavros. How are you?"

"Never better."

"I'm glad to hear it. Is Andreas still asleep?"

"No," sounded a familiar voice behind her. She swung around to discover him standing there in a sage-colored polo shirt and white shorts. There couldn't be a more attractive man anywhere in the Cyclades. His slate eyes collided with hers. "I've been waiting for you and the babies to appear. Let's eat. I'm ravenous."

"I'm hungry myself," she admitted. "It must be this gorgeous air." Andreas sat down next to her. Gabi tried to act natural, but after her dreams of him it was close to impossible.

Andreas studied her for a moment. "How did you sleep?"

Was this god from Olympus psychic, too?

"Would you believe these two didn't start crying until seven-thirty? It's the first time I haven't had to get up in the middle of the night. The pediatrician said it would happen when the time was right. Isn't it strange how they both did it at the same time?"

His compelling mouth broke into a lopsided smile. "My mother could tell you endless stories about the mystifying aspect of twins."

"I don't doubt it." She would love to meet the mother of this extraordinary man, but held back from telling him so. Near the end of their meal he chuckled over Nikos, who gave a big yawn. In the next breath he got up and took the twins out of their carry-cots. Propping them in either arm, he moved over to the windows. "What do you think of this sight, guys?"

Gabi had been concentrating so hard on Andreas, she could tell him that the sight of him standing there holding his nephews was the most spectacular one in all Greece. Terrified to realize how emotionally involved she'd become with him, she found it a struggle not to let him know it.

When she could finally tear her gaze away, she noticed the cruiser was anchored off an unreal white outcropping of elongated rocks set against a brilliant blue sea. She stood up and joined him. "What is this place?"

"Sarakiniko, an Arabic word."

"It looks like a moonscape."

"That's what it's famous for. When we were boys, Leon and I would come here to play space aliens with our friends."

She laughed. "That beats the neighborhood park." Andreas's backyard was unlike any other. "Every time you show me a new place, I think it's the most fabulous spot around. I'll never be able to thank you enough for this tour. I'm very lucky."

He cast her a sideward glance. "Seeing everything through your eyes has taken me back to happier days and times. I'm the one indebted to you, so let's agree we're even."

Once again she sensed he was brooding. If he'd heard from Leon, he would have told her. His change in demeanor had everything to do with his brother.

Gabi knew most men stuck in this unique situation would have left her to her own devices while she waited for word from his brother. Not Andreas. His unselfishness meant he'd put his own needs aside, but it was wearing on him. She wouldn't allow this to happen again.

For the next while they lazed on deck and played with the babies. To convince him he wasn't the sole meaning of her existence she phoned her mother to let her know she and the children were fine. She hoped that if she played it breezy in front of him, he wouldn't suspect how on fire she still was for him.

Her mom was delighted to learn the boys had

slept through the night. In front of Andreas she raved about her sightseeing trip and his kindness, then promised to phone again when she knew more about Leon's plans. He could probably see through her attempt to keep everything light and above board, but she had to try.

By the time she hung up, they were coming into port at Apollonia. Since Andreas was still having fun with the babies, she excused herself and went below to pack up the few things in her cabin. She found Stavros and thanked him.

Within a half hour Andreas had driven them back to the house. While he helped her and the twins inside, she sensed he had other matters on his mind. As he was bringing in the last bag, she met him at the door.

"Stop right there. You've done enough." She took the bag from him. "I had the time of my life. Now go. I know you'll get back to me when you have any news."

Gabi felt his gaze travel over her, turning her body feverish. He seemed reluctant to leave. "Promise me you'll phone if you need anything."

His entreaty spoken in that husky tone sent a weakness to her legs. She rubbed her palms against her hips nervously. "You know I will. Now I've got to take care of the babies."

"Before you do that, I need this." In the next breath he pulled her into his arms and started kissing her again. Caught off guard, she was helpless to stop him. Gabi had been dying for his touch since last night. Without conscious thought she slid her hands up his chest and encircled his neck, needing to get closer to him.

He was such a gorgeous man. With every caress her senses spiraled. The heat he created was like a fever in her blood. Another minute and she would beg him to stay. Through sheer strength of will she wrenched her mouth from his and eased away from him, breathing in gulps of air.

"I'll be back. Miss me a little." With another hard kiss to her trembling mouth, he strode off. She shut the door and fell against it while she waited for him to drive away.

As soon as she couldn't hear the car motor any longer, she made fresh bottles of formula, then put the twins in their stroller and headed out the door for a long walk. If her life depended on it, she couldn't have stayed in the house another second, not when she was feeling this kind of pent-up energy. She didn't plan to come back until she'd visited every shop in the village and had worn herself out.

At noon the next day Gabi left the house again, this time taking the twins with her to enjoy lunch in a delightful little restaurant she'd passed last evening. It was a good thing Andreas hadn't come back.

She blushed to realize how wantonly she'd responded to him at the door. Twice now she'd been playing with fire, but only she was going to get burned if she continued to let it happen every time he got near her.

During the delicious meal, the babies created a minor sensation with customers and staff alike. On her way out the door several tourists asked if they could take their picture because they thought the boys were so angelic.

Gabi supposed it didn't matter as long as

no one knew they were the sons of Leonides Simonides. In that case their pictures would show up in the newspaper and on television.

Before long she reached the path to the house. As she was about to open the door she heard a female voice call to her. She turned around to see the manager come hurrying up to her. "I'm glad you're back. You have a visitor who's been waiting for a while. She's in the office."

"Who is it?"

"Mrs. Simonides."

Her heart pounded an extra beat. Deline? Was it possible? Where was Leon? Or maybe it was Andreas's mother. Had he dropped her off with the intention of coming by for her later? She could hardly breathe at the thought of seeing him again.

"While I take the children inside, would you please show her over here, Lena?"

"Of course." She rushed off.

Gabi looked down at the children. "Come on, you cute little things. Someone has come to see you. I want you to look your very best."

After wheeling them inside, she brought out

the big quilt and put it on the living-room floor where they could stretch out while she changed them. With that accomplished she put them in their white and yellow stretchy suits. The colors brought out the warm tone of their olive complexions. She kissed their necks. "Umm, you smell sweet."

When she heard the knock, she jumped up and darted over to the door to open it. The tall, slender brunette beauty on the other side couldn't be much older than Gabi's twenty-five years. She'd worn makeup but it didn't disguise the telltale signs of pain. Gabi detected a distinct pallor and her eyelids were swollen from too much crying.

"You must be Deline." She spoke first. Her heart ached for the other woman who'd found the courage to come and at least see the children.

"Yes. I understand you're Thea Paulos's half sister Gabriella."

"That's right. Please come in." She had a dozen questions, but didn't ask one. This was too significant a moment to intrude on Deline's personal agony. She followed her into the living room where the twins were lying on their backs making infant sounds. Their compact bodies were in constant motion.

Gabi's lungs constricted while she waited for a reaction from Leon's wife. It wasn't long in coming.

A pained cry escaped her lips and she sank into one end of the sofa as if her legs could no longer support her. Tears gushed down her cheeks. "They look exactly like him, but they should have been *our* children," came her tortured whisper.

By now moisture had bathed Gabi's face. "I'm so sorry, Deline. I wouldn't blame you if you hated me for contacting Andreas. When I went to his office, I thought h-he was their father," she stammered.

"Andreas told me everything." Deline shook her head. "But a situation like this would never have happened to him. Unlike Leon, he doesn't lose his head when he's down or upset. That's why he was made the head of the company over Leon after their father suffered his heart attack."

"I didn't realize." Gabi knew so little really.

"When Andreas is married, his wife will be able to trust him to the death."

The blood pounded in her ears. "Is he getting married soon?"

"Irena's expecting a proposal any day now. She's his girlfriend and my best friend. Her family owns one of the major newspapers here in Greece. She heads the travel section department."

All of a sudden Gabi had to reach for the nearest chair and sit down. Swallowing hard, she said, "Will they be married soon?"

"Irena's hoping so. He's in Athens with her this weekend."

Gabi had to fight not to break down hysterically. It appeared Andreas and Leon had more in common than Deline knew.

Last night Andreas had kissed her senseless. If Gabi hadn't pulled away when she did, she'd have made the same mistake as Thea. When he'd told her he didn't have a wife, she'd taken it to mean he didn't have a romantic interest of any kind at the moment. What a naïve fool she was!

Yet none of it mattered in light of what Deline was going through. Gabi was being incredibly selfish to be thinking about herself at a time like this.

"How can I help you, Deline? I'd like to."

She looked down at the children. "You can't. I've loved Leon forever and always wanted his baby so badly, but it never happened. Now that I'm going to divorce him, there won't ever be that possibility. Life's so unfair." Sobs shook her body.

Gabi's heart sank to her feet. "I agree. My father lost his daughter early, and Thea didn't live long enough to raise her babies. I'm convinced that if she hadn't developed a heart problem, she would never have told me anything and this situation wouldn't have arisen."

"But it did," Deline stated flatly, "and Leon wants his sons, which is only natural. He's told his family, so that's it." She jumped up from the couch. "This morning he came to my parents' home and begged me to fly here and see the children before I did anything else.

"I know what he's hoping for, but he doesn't understand. Even if I wanted to stay with him and was willing to give our marriage one more chance, I don't see *me* in their countenances." Her voice broke. "I'm afraid I'll always see her and resent them even though they're innocent in all this."

Gabi felt such a wrench, she got up and put her arms around Deline. "I admire you for your gut honesty," she cried softly. "I can't tell you how sorry I am."

Deline relaxed enough to hug her back. When they finally let go she asked, "What will you do now?"

"As soon as Leon comes for the children, I'm going back to Crete and then on to the States. My job is waiting for me."

"What do you do?"

"I'm a manager at an advertising agency. It's a fascinating business I like very much." For the twins' sake if nothing else, she had to keep giving herself that pep talk in front of them. If she ever truly broke down, she might not get herself back together again. "Do you work?"

"Not yet, but I have a friend who has offered to let me work in a hotel gift shop. I'm thinking of doing that so I don't fall apart."

Good for her! Gabi could relate. Deline wasn't only wonderful, she had a backbone. "I wish you the very best. I hope you know I mean that."

While they'd been talking, Kris started to whimper. Gabi picked him up to comfort him.

Deline studied her for a moment while dashing the tears off her face. "I was prepared not to like you, but having met you I've discovered that's impossible."

Gabi's eyes filled again. Leon was losing a perfectly fabulous woman. How sad that he and Thea had ever met. Because of that pregnancy, Thea was no longer alive. But following that thought, if they'd never gotten together, there'd be no babies. She would never have met Andreas. No matter how hurt she was,

Gabi could never wish the three of them didn't exist.

She walked Deline to the door. "Did you fly here?"

"In the helicopter with Leon. He's gone on to the villa. When he knows I've left the island, he'll be over."

Things were moving fast. "I hope you have a safe flight."

Before she could respond, the baby hiccupped, proving a distraction for Deline, who couldn't help examining his dear little face. "Which one is he?"

"Kris."

"The one who has to have the heart surgery?"

"Yes."

"He looks well."

"I know, but he tires more easily and fusses more than Nikos. He's a little smaller, too. When they're grown, he'll probably be an inch shorter. The doctor said this first operation is going to make a big difference."

Her lower lip quivered. "H-he's so sweet." Her voice caught before she turned away with an

abruptness Gabi understood. "I have to go." She
hurried off.

"Take care," she called after her.

Oh, Deline...

CHAPTER SIX

WITH a heavy heart Gabi closed the door. After feeding the babies, she put them down for their nap before checking her watch. It was ten after two. She phoned her mother, but all she got was her voice mail. Gabi left a message that she'd be returning to Heraklion without the children.

While she waited for Leon to come for his boys, she checked airline schedules and ferry crossings to Crete. There wouldn't be another flight out of the island airport until tomorrow, but there was a ferry to Kimolos leaving from the pier at five-thirty. From there she would take another ferry to Heraklion.

She needed one more day to be with her parents and get her packing done. Then she'd fly to Athens and make a connecting flight to Washington, D.C. Without the twins to care for, it was imperative she put an ocean between her and Andreas.

A knock on the door broke her concentration. "Gabi? Are you in there?"

It was Leon's voice. She hurried across the room to open it. He looked worse than Deline, as if he hadn't slept in days. "Come in. Your wife said you'd be over."

He followed her into the living room. "I'm not going to have a wife much longer."

There was nothing she could say to comfort him on that score. He knew better than to ask her questions about their conversation since she couldn't answer them out of respect for Deline. "But you do have two little babies who need their daddy. What plans have you made?"

"For the time being I'm going to keep them with me at my villa here. Estelle, the house-keeper, is going to take over as their nanny until I can find a permanent one. Mother will help. The family is around right now, turning one of the bedrooms into a nursery. Everyone's anxious to help me get them settled. Needless to say, my parents are eager to love their newest grandchildren."

"I'm sure they are."

"Gabi?" His bloodshot eyes had gone moist. "I'm aware of how much you and your parents love them. This has to be a very difficult moment for you."

"It is. I won't lie to you about that, but you gave them life. They need you more than my folks and I need them. The sooner you take over, the sooner they're going to become yours, heart and soul."

"You know my home will always be open to you."

"Of course. In two months I plan to fly back to Crete to see my parents for a week. By then Kris will have had his operation and be recovered in time for all of us to have a reunion."

"I'll be looking forward to it. We'll have a family party where everyone can get acquainted."

Gabi wondered how she would live until she saw them or Andreas again. "The next time you're with your brother, please tell him thank you for making the arrangements here. It's been a lovely vacation for me."

"Andreas is the greatest friend a person could have."

I know.

Together they packed up the children's things and put them in his car. Leon had already installed two infant carseats in the back. Then came time to carry the children out of the house and buckle them in.

Throughout the process they stayed asleep, not having any idea that the next time they woke up, they'd be home with their daddy for the rest of their lives. And Andreas would always be their loving uncle…

Such lives they were going to lead being the sons of a Simonides!

She was thrilled for them. For herself, she was dying inside from too many losses in one day. *Don't lose it yet, Gabi. Remember why you sought out Andreas in the first place.*

Leon came around and hugged her hard. "You've been a guardian angel all this time. I'm never going to forget. Before I go, let's program in each other's cell-phone numbers. I'm afraid I'll be calling you pretty constantly until I get the hang of being a father. The children will be wanting you all the time."

"For a day or two maybe."

Gabi ran back in the house to get her phone. In a minute they were both set and there was nothing else to detain him. He climbed in behind the steering wheel. She shut the door. Leon pressed her hand one more time before turning on the motor.

Leave now before my little darlings open their eyes.

She waved until everything became a blur.

The minute the helicopter touched down on the helipad behind the villa on Milos, Andreas climbed out. He'd just come from Irena's, where he'd told her everything. She deserved to know about the twins and the strange circumstances that had brought Gabi into his life.

Even in her pain, Irena demonstrated a rare graciousness before he said goodbye. Now he was anxious to find his brother. He assumed everyone was out at the pool enjoying dinner. After he ate, he'd disappear with his brother.

As he drew closer he could hear his family talking. They sounded more animated than usual. He couldn't help but be curious over the reason why. When he descended the last flight of steps, he saw their large clan congregated around Leon and his parents. To his shock they were holding Kris and Nikos, but the babies weren't happy about it.

Andreas's heart thundered in his chest. He jerked his head to the side looking for Gabi. He felt as if it had been weeks instead of hours since he'd last seen her, but there was no sign of her.

Leon caught his glance and came striding toward him. He pulled Andreas over to the wall where they could talk in private.

"As you can see, the secret is out now. The family knows everything."

Andreas had to admit he was relieved. Now he didn't have to bear the burden of it alone. "Did Deline get a look at the twins?"

"This afternoon. Then she flew back to Athens. I'll be receiving divorce papers shortly."

Unfortunately he'd been afraid of that. "Where's Gabi?"

"On her way home."

It appeared Andreas had just missed her. "You mean the resort."

"No. I mean the States. She said she'd be back in two months for a visit with her folks. That's when I plan to get both our families together."

Two months?

His guts froze. "You mean she's already left Milos?"

Leon stared at him in surprise. "As far as I know."

"And you didn't stop her?"

His brother blinked. "Take it easy, Andreas. Why would I do that?"

"Why *wouldn't* you?" he fired back. "Gabi's been their mother for the last three months. She must be out of her mind with grief right now."

"I'm sure she is, but we both agreed it had to be this way so I could bond with my sons. In this case a complete break was necessary if the babies are going to look to me for their needs now."

Andreas couldn't argue with her logic or Leon's, but after the brief intimacy they'd shared the knowledge that Gabi had left Greece made him feel as if his tether had come loose from the mother ship and he was left to float out into the dark void.

"She asked me to thank you for the vacation arrangements in Apollonia."

He rubbed the back of his neck while he tried to take it all in. When he thought of her response on the beach, and at the door yesterday… Didn't it mean anything to her?

"Bro?" Leon whispered. "Did you hear what I said?"

Yes. Andreas heard him, but he couldn't waste any more time talking. "Leon? Do me a favor and make my excuses to the family while I go inside for a minute. I'll be right back."

While his brother stood there looking visibly perplexed, Andreas raced up the side steps. When he was out of sight of the others he called the resort. "I'd like to speak to Lena. This is Andreas Simonides."

"One moment please." He paced until he heard her voice. "Kyrie Simonides? What can I do for you?"

"I understand Ms. Turner checked out today. Did you order a car for her so she could be driven to the airport?"

"Not to the airport. She went to the pier to get the ferry."

That ferry only went to Kimolos.

His adrenaline surged. "Thank you. That's all I needed to know."

He hung up. Gabi would have to stay there overnight until there was a different ferry to Athens tomorrow. He had time to make plans.

With his pulse racing, he rejoined the family. Two extremely miserable babies were being passed around. They were looking for the one beautiful, familiar golden angel who didn't make up part of the dark-haired Simonides family.

No one—not his sisters, his mother or Estelle could calm them. Leon had to take over, but they still weren't completely comforted. Andreas knew in his gut Gabi wasn't in nearly as good a shape as the twins were.

His mother shot him a curious glance. "Where did you go? Why isn't Irena with you?"

Now was not the time to discuss his breakup or the reason behind it. "She couldn't make it. I had an important phone call to deal with."

"Have you eaten yet?"

"I'm not hungry."

She shook her head. "Your brother told us the saga about the twins and the major role you and Gabriella Turner have played in all of it. You're a remarkable son, Andreas. I love you for your loyalty to him."

"Deline's destroyed all over again."

His mother nodded. "I'm afraid she might not be able to deal with his babies, not when she wants one so badly herself." Her eyes filled with fresh tears. "But the boys are so adorable. It's uncanny how much they resemble you and Leon at that age."

"They have the look of their mother, too. I saw pictures when I was at the consulate."

"The Turner family must be devastated over

their loss. Your father and I would like to meet them."

"I'll arrange it." *Just as soon as I catch up to Gabi.*

The splotchy face and swollen eyes that looked back from the hotel-room mirror made Gabi wince. She could only hope that by the time she went aboard the ferry taking her to Heraklion later in the day, all traces of the terrible night she'd just lived through would be gone.

She finished dressing in jeans and a white sleeveless blouse. Her hair, still damp from its shampoo, was already curling. The heat would dry her out in no time. With a coat of coral lipstick, she felt a little more presentable to face the day.

After having given Leon all the babies' things yesterday, she had only her overnight bag to carry down to the pier surrounded with its assembly of fishing boats and other craft. Small groups of tourists were slowly making their way to the same embarkation point where they could see the ferry entering the port.

She hadn't been anywhere without the children for so long, she felt empty. Were they missing her? Her eyelids burned. The only way her parents were handling the loss was because they had each other. They were the great loves in each other's lives.

When she'd thought she'd be raising the twins, she hadn't met Andreas yet and had been glad she was single. Now she had nothing left except her dreams of a god who'd turned out to be too human after all. More than ever she was eager to get back to her career.

"Gabi?"

She thought she was hearing things and kept walking. When her name was called out a second time, she slowed down and turned around. By then it was too late to stifle the cry that sprang from her throat. Her overnight bag dropped to the ground.

Andreas studied her tear-ravaged face. "I thought so," his voice rasped.

Her mouth had gone dry at the sight of him. He looked impossibly handsome wearing white cargo pants and a blue crewneck shirt with the sleeves pushed up to the elbows.

"If something's wrong with the children, why didn't Leon call me? He has my number."

He scrutinized her for a moment. "Whatever happened to hello? How are you? Isn't this a beautiful day!"

Heat spilled into her cheeks, but she didn't look away. "A man with your kind of responsibilities doesn't show up at an obscure port off the beaten track unless there's a dire emergency."

"That's not always true or fair." He stood there with stunning nonchalance. "You're suddenly making judgments about me. What's changed since we last saw each other?"

For him, nothing. Though he had a serious girlfriend right now, he enjoyed being the quintessential playboy up to the very end. Why not? Little did he know the experience with Rand had taught her two could dance to that tune.

"Absolutely nothing. Last week I told you that if Leon decided to claim the children, I had to get back to my job."

He rubbed the side of his hard jaw absently.

"I'm the one who brought you to Milos. Why didn't you at least wait until I could make arrangements to get you back to Crete?"

She pasted on a phony smile. "Andreas—I'm a businesswoman, remember? I'm capable of looking out for myself."

His expression tautened even more. "Didn't it occur to you I wanted to do that for you?"

The fact that he'd shown up here proved he was hoping to pick up where they'd left off at the beach. If his girlfriend knew about the other women he played around with, then she had a high tolerance level. Gabi wasn't made the same way.

"It's not a case of occurring to me. You're probably the most generous person I've ever known. But you're also the head of your family's company. Now that Leon's been united with his children, you and I have other fish to fry, as we Americans say. I'm due for a promotion as soon as I return to Alexandria, so it's imperative I leave Greece on the next flight out."

His silvery eyes bored into hers. "Will one more day matter in the scheme of things?"

Yes, considering the convulsion he'd set off by his unexpected presence here. "Since my boss is expecting me, I'm afraid so. Now if you'll excuse me, people are starting to board the ferry."

"Let them," he declared. "My boat will take you wherever you want to go."

She sustained his gaze without flinching. Andreas had an agenda and insisted on taking her to her parents, so there was no point in fighting him. If she kept her wits about her, she ought to be able to handle a few more hours alone with him. Play along for a little while longer. That was the key.

"Okay. I give up. Hello, Andreas. It's lovely to see you again. What brings you to this island on such a beautiful summer morning?"

Laughter rumbled out of him. "That's better."

"I'm glad you think so." The charisma of the man had the power to raise her temperature. "My plan is to go back to Heraklion. I need to pack the rest of my things before I fly home."

He picked up her overnight bag. "Come with

me and we'll reach Crete long before the ferry gets there."

Andreas walked her in another direction toward a sleek-looking jet boat tied up in one of the slips. The Simonides family had a different vessel for every occasion. For this trip it was going to be just the two of them. Though she forbade it, she couldn't stop the thrill of excitement that spread through her body to be with him again. She had to be some kind of masochist.

After helping her on board, he handed her a life jacket and told her to put it on. While she buckled up, he undid the ropes and jumped in, taking his place at the wheel. Before he could turn on the engine, she handed him a life jacket. "What's sauce for the goose..." she teased. "Do you know the expression?"

"I know a better one." He smiled back. "Never argue with a woman holding a weapon." He slanted her an amused glance before taking it from her and putting it on his hard-muscled frame. She felt relief knowing that if, heaven help them, something happened on the way to Crete, he was wearing a floating device, too.

The cold, implacable head of the Simonides corporation she'd first confronted at his office was so far removed from the relaxed man driving the boat, she had trouble connecting the two. Before she knew it, they were idling out to sea at a wakeless speed.

"How long are you going to keep me in suspense about what really brought you here this morning?"

Andreas didn't pretend to misunderstand. "Not long." He engaged the gears and the boat burst across the water like a surfaced torpedo.

Gabi had to be happy with that explanation. She *was* happy. Too happy to be with him when he didn't know what it meant to be faithful to one woman. Gabi wished she didn't care and could give in to her desire without counting the cost.

Deline was a much better woman than Gabi. She'd forgiven Leon his one-night stand with Thea. *Until she'd found out about the twins...*

Resigned to her fate—at least until they

reached Heraklion—Gabi put her head back to feel the sun on her face. Every so often the boat kicked up spray, dappling her skin with fine droplets of water. She kept her eyes closed in an attempt to rein in her exhilaration.

The problem was, she'd fallen irrevocably in love with Andreas, the deep, painful kind that would never go away. But she'd made up her mind he would never know he was the great love of her life. Nor would she ever dare to say it out loud. An ordinary mortal reaching for the unattainable might bring on the mockery of the gods.

"Tell me something honestly, Gabi. How wedded are you to returning to your old job?"

His question jolted her back to the real world. She sat up, eyeing him through shuttered lids to keep out the blinding sun. "I'm very wedded. Besides being stimulating, it provides me a comfortable living with the promise of great things in the future. Why do you ask?"

He cut the motor, immediately creating silence except for the lapping of water against the hull. In a deft motion he left his seat long enough to produce a couple of sodas from the cooler. After handing her one, he sat down again with his well-honed body turned toward her.

"Thank you. I didn't realize I was thirsty until now."

His eyes, a solid metal-gray at the moment, met hers over the rim of his drink. "I know what you mean." An odd nuance in his low voice caused her to believe he was referring to something else. Memories of the two of them communicating in the most elemental of ways on that beach never left her mind. Trembling, she looked away.

"What do you recall about my receptionist?"

The question was so strange, she thought she hadn't heard him right, but Andreas never said or did anything without a reason. "I suppose I thought she was firm, but fair...even kind in her own way."

"An excellent description," he murmured. "Anna's going to be seventy on her next birthday. She worked for my father forty-five years and never married."

"They must have been a perfect match for her

to stay in his employ that long." Gabi imagined the woman had been madly in love with the senior Simonides. If he had a tenth of his son's brilliance and vitality, it all made perfect sense.

"When he stepped down, I kept her on with the intention of asking her to train a new receptionist before I let her go. However, after one day of working with her, I realized what a treasure she was and I refused to consider breaking in anyone else."

Gabi swallowed the rest of her drink. "If it hadn't been for her, the twins would still be without their father. For that alone, I like her without really knowing her."

She heard his sharp intake of breath. "Being a receptionist is only one of Anna's jobs. In a word, she's the keeper of the flame. Do you understand what I mean?"

"I think so," Gabi said with conviction. "She's a paragon of the virtues you admire most."

He nodded gravely. "But she needs to retire and get the knee replacement she's been putting off."

"I noticed her limping."

"It's getting worse every day. The trouble is, I've despaired of finding anyone else like her. Then I met *you*." His piercing glance rested on her, reminding her of something he'd said to her a week ago.

If you were looking for a job, I'd hire you as my personal assistant on your integrity and discretion alone.

The worst nightmare she could conceive of was upon her. She knew exactly where this conversation was going and shook her head.

"Before you refuse me outright," he said, "I'm only suggesting that I could use your help while I look around the company for the right person to replace her. It could take me several months. You'll be given your own furnished apartment on the floor below my office. There's a restaurant on the next floor down for the staff."

"Andreas—" she blurted almost angrily. "What's this really about?"

"I don't want you to leave Greece until we know Kris's heart operation is successful.

If there are complications, you'll want to be here."

She didn't want to be reminded of that possibility. "I'm praying everything will go well, but if it doesn't, I'll fly over on the spot."

"That's not good enough."

What was going on inside him? She knew his request couldn't be for personal reasons. Besides his girlfriend, there were legions of women who'd love a fling with him. "Why?"

He seemed fascinated by the pulse throbbing in her throat. "I just came from being with the family. The babies were out of control. We both know they were looking for you." *They were?* "Let's be honest. With the operation coming up, Leon's going to need you. I know it in my gut."

Gabi bowed her head. "They'll get over the separation in a few days and cling to him."

"I don't believe that, and neither do you." Andreas leaned closer to her. "These things take time. I know how much you love the boys. Admit you're dying inside after having to give them up."

"Of course I am." The tears started spurting. Too late she covered her face with her hands.

"*Gabi...*" Andreas whispered in a compassionate voice.

"When Thea asked me to find a couple who would adopt the boys, it killed me because *I* wanted to be the one to take over. She didn't know that by then I was prepared to give up my career for them. But the law forced me to come to you."

"Thank God it did!" In a sinuous movement Andreas pulled her into his arms. At first she remained stiff, but his gentle rocking broke down every defense and she ended up sobbing against his broad shoulder.

"I know how much you love them," he murmured into her silky curls. "That's why I don't want you to leave. Stay and work for me until Kris has recovered fully from his operation. You and I can visit the twins after work every few days. That way everyone will be happy and it won't interfere with the bonding going on between them and their father."

When she realized she'd be content to stay

like this forever, she eased away from him and wiped her eyes with the backs of her hands.

Eventually she glanced at him, never having realized gray eyes could be so warm. His love of the twins produced that translucent glow. "When you put it that way, you manage to exorcize all the demons. Only Andreas Simonides can make everything sound so simple and reasonable, even if it isn't."

"That's all I needed to hear. The matter's settled."

No. It's not. "Nothing's settled. First I have to talk to my boss and determine if that promotion will still be waiting for me if I get back at a later date."

"After knowing you a week, I can guarantee he'll move mountains to accommodate you in order to get you in the end."

Andreas said whatever needed to be said in order to accomplish his objective. That was why he was the head of the family business. There was just one problem. She couldn't figure out his objective. She knew he loved the twins, but he was after something more.

"Tell me the real reason you're asking me to temp for you. By your answer, I'll know if you're telling me the truth or not."

"You're not just anyone. You're the twins' aunt. There's no reason why you shouldn't be able to peek in on them from time to time. That's hard to do from across the ocean." A compelling smile broke out on his striking face. "I want to peek with you."

Andreas...

She averted her eyes. "That's the wrong answer."

"It's the only one I have," he answered with enviable calm.

"You mean the only one you're willing to offer me. Without knowing the truth, I can't stay in Greece even if my boss were willing to give me more time away."

His smile faded. "I didn't know there was more truth to tell unless it's my guilt."

She blinked. "About what?"

He eyed her intently. "About everything. It's my fault my brother's marriage is in trouble again. If I'd left everything alone after you walked out of my office, they wouldn't be headed for divorce and the twins would be in Virginia leading perfectly contented lives with you."

"Except that I couldn't have adopted them."

"They'd have still been yours, Gabi."

"And after they grew up and demanded to know about their father, what then? If I admitted that I'd known his name all along, they might never forgive me."

A strange sound came out of his throat. "You've just put your finger on my greatest nightmare. If I'd kept the secret of the twins over the years *knowing* Leon and his wife could never have children, I wouldn't have been able to forgive myself for playing god with my brother's life."

It was Gabi's turn to moan.

He reached out and grasped her hands. "The truth is, you and I are up to our necks in this mess together. Leon needs our help for a little while longer."

She sucked in her breath. "But you don't really need an assistant."

"Actually I do. Anna's got to get that knee operated on right away."

"You could hire any number of secretaries in your company to replace her."

"I could, but I thought one of the reasons you were leaving Crete was so your parents could get back to the lives they were leading before Thea became ill."

"You're right," she confessed quietly.

"By the time you leave my employ, I'll be hiring a permanent assistant." He kissed the back of her hands before letting them go. A tingling sensation coursed through Gabi's sensitized body and lingered for the rest of the trip to Heraklion.

CHAPTER SEVEN

THE blood donation area of the hospital in Athens had continual traffic. Gabi looked over at Andreas. Both of them were stretched out side by side on cots giving blood. They'd taken the day off from work. It was a good thing since they'd had to wait at least an hour after arriving there before their turn was announced.

In preparation for today she'd eaten a good breakfast and had forced down fluids. Before bringing her to the hospital where Kris would be having his surgery, Andreas had instructed the limo driver to drop them off at a fabulous restaurant in the Plaka for lunch. But instead of ordering the specialty of the house, they'd eaten iron-rich spinach salad followed by sirloin steak.

Andreas was remarkable. In the short time she'd been working for him, she'd learned that when he did something, he always did it right and thoroughly. She loved him with a vengeance. If Kris weren't facing an operation, Andreas wouldn't have asked her to stay on and none of this would be happening.

"This is kind of like lying on the beach at Papafragas."

For him to mention that night—out of the blue—when she'd lost almost every inhibition in his arms came as such a surprise, she almost fell off the cot.

"It's not as warm," she murmured.

"No, and we're not alone. It's a good thing we don't have to swim the length of that fjord later. We're not supposed to do any strenuous activity for the rest of the day. I wouldn't be able to save you."

In spite of that bittersweet memory, she couldn't help but laugh. "Then what are we going to do?"

"I'll tell the chauffeur to drive us back to the office and we'll watch TV in your apartment while we take it easy."

"If you get lightheaded, the long couch is

yours," she quipped, but the second the words came out, she regretted saying anything. Since the day he'd shown it to her, he'd never asked to come inside and she'd never invited him. To cover her tracks she asked, "Do you ever watch TV?"

"All the time."

"You're joking—"

He chuckled. "Leon and I are sports nuts."

"I can believe *that*, but when do you find the time?"

"My iPhone. Broadband is everywhere and performs almost every trick known to technological mankind."

"Aha! So in between important phone calls and meetings, you're watching soccer?"

"Or basketball or the NFL."

"How about NASCAR? The Grand Prix?"

"Love it all."

She frowned. "And here I thought you were different."

His smile was too much. "What do *you* watch?"

"When I'm in the States and have time, the

History Channel and cooking shows, British comedies and mysteries. I also like bull-riding."

"You're a fan of the rodeo?"

"When I was in college, a friend of mine attending there asked me to go back to Austin with her during our two-week break. We met a couple of cowboys and got talked into going to one. I've been hooked ever since."

He stared at her as if trying to find a way into her soul. "On a certain cowboy?"

"For a time I was," she answered honestly, "but the illness passed."

"Have there been many?"

"Many what?" She knew exactly what he meant.

"Illnesses."

"Probably half a dozen." She didn't want to talk about old boyfriends. The man lying near her made every male she'd ever known fade into insignificance. "Andreas? Speaking of illness, what did Kris's heart surgeon tell Leon when he took him in for his checkup yesterday? You went with him, but you acted differently when you came back to the office."

"Did I?"

"You know you did. If you're trying to spare me, please don't."

Suddenly the curtain was swept aside and two hospital staff came in to finish up and unhook them. "You're all done." They both sat up and put their legs on the floor. "Take your time. There are refreshments outside before you leave the hospital."

When they were alone again, Gabi slid off the cot and turned to him. "I'm still waiting for an answer."

By now Andreas had rolled down his shirt-sleeve and was on his feet. "The doctor couldn't promise the operation would be risk free."

"Of course not. No operation is."

"My brother's dealing with too many emotions right now."

They all were. She sensed Andreas was se-cretly worried, but he hid it well. "On top of Leon's pain, taking care of the twins is physically exhausting work no matter how sweet they are."

His eyes were almost slumberous as they looked at her. "We need time off from our fears, too. Since there's nothing more we can do for the moment, let's go home and relax."

She watched him shrug into his jacket. He sounded as if he meant that they would actually go back to her apartment and spend the rest of the day together, but it was out of the question. Andreas had a playful side that could throw her off guard at unexpected moments, but from the time Deline had told her he had a serious girl-friend, Gabi refused to play.

After they'd been served juice and rolls, the limo took them to the office. They rode his private elevator to her floor. Gabi's heart thudded heavily as they walked across the foyer to her suite.

She opened the door, then turned to him. "Thank you for accompanying me this far in case I fainted, but as you can see I'm fine. If you're feeling dizzy, there's a very comfortable couch to lie down on in the reception room of your office." A smile broke the corner of her mouth. "I know because I spent half a day on it waiting for you to give me an audience."

She heard him inhale quickly, as if he were out of breath and needed more air. "I'm sorry you were forced to wait so long."

"I'm not," she said brightly. "It gave me an opportunity to watch Anna at work. On that day who would have guessed I'd end up filling in temporarily after she left?"

When he still made no move to leave, she said, "Thank you for giving blood with me, Andreas. I'm glad I didn't have to do it alone. See you in the morning and we'll plan that big company party you want to give for Anna after she's recovered from her knee surgery."

Before the weakness invading her body smothered the voice telling her not to let him get near enough to touch her, she stepped inside and started to close the door.

"Not so fast." Andreas had put his foot there, making it impossible to shut it. Quick as lightning he stepped inside and closed it. Her heart thumped so hard, she was afraid he could hear it.

"What is it?"

"What do you think?" he demanded in a silky voice.

Uh-oh. Gabi backed away from him. "I—I'm sure I don't know," she stammered.

He moved toward her. "When I left you at the resort on Apollonia after our night at Papafragas, I held a woman in my arms who was with me all the way. In the blink of an eye I learned she'd left the island. When I went after that woman and found her, she'd changed. Since then I've been waiting for her to re-emerge, but she hasn't. Now I want to know why."

She smoothed her palms against her hips, a gesture his piercing gaze followed while she tried to think up an answer. Unless it was the truth, nothing would satisfy him, but in doing so she would give herself away.

As the silence lengthened a grimace marred his handsome features. "At the hospital you admitted there was no other man in your life, or is that a lie and it's your boss you're in love with?"

Gabi had a hard time believing she'd injured his pride by playing hard to get, because *that* was all this interrogation could possibly be about.

"No," she finally answered with every bit of control she could muster. "Like you, I don't have a significant other I'm keeping secrets from." She'd said it on purpose to watch for the slightest guilty reaction from him. Now was the time for him to admit his involvement with the woman Deline had mentioned, but nothing was forthcoming.

"If that's true, why do you rush away from me the second our business day is over? How come we never share a meal unless it's on Milos while we're checking on the twins?" His eyes narrowed on her mouth. "Have I suddenly become repulsive to you?"

She was aghast. "I'm not going to dignify that absurd question with an answer." If anyone were listening, they'd think he was her husband listing the latest problem in their marriage.

"Then prove it. I told you I'd like to spend the rest of the afternoon with you. We can do it here or at my penthouse."

There was no putting him off. She bit her lip. "Well, as long as you're here, y—"

"My thoughts exactly." He finished her sentence and removed his jacket, tossing it over a side chair. "When we get hungry later, we'll have the restaurant send something up."

She got that excited sensation in her midriff. "Excuse me for a moment."

"Take all the time you need to freshen up. I'm not going anywhere."

That was what she was afraid of as she darted from the living room. The second she saw herself in the bathroom mirror she groaned to see her cheeks were filled with hectic color. After giving blood, she was shocked by her body's betrayal.

When she returned a few minutes later her feet came to a standstill. Andreas had stretched out on her couch with his eyes closed. He'd turned on television to a made-for-TV Greek movie.

He was so gorgeous, she didn't dare move or

breathe in case he sensed she was there and caught her feasting her eyes on him. Every part of his male facial structure was perfect. From his wavy black hair to the long, hard-muscled length of his powerful anatomy, he was a superb specimen. But it was the core of the remarkable human beneath that radiated throughout, bringing alive the true essence of what a real man should be.

Maybe it was the combination of giving blood and the many hours of work he'd been packing into each day so they could spend time with the twins. Whatever, it all seemed to have taken its toll. She could tell from the way he was breathing that he'd fallen asleep.

He would never know how much she wanted to lie down and wrap her arms around him, never letting him go, but she couldn't. Feeling tired herself, she lay down on the small couch facing him so she could watch him as he slept.

The movie played on, but she had no idea what it was about. Her lids grew heavy. When next she became cognizant of her surroundings,

Andreas had just set a tray of sandwiches and coffee on the table.

Surprised at how deeply she'd slept, she took a minute to clear her head before she sat up. Her watch said five to six! She glanced at Andreas. "How long have you been awake?"

"About twenty minutes. It's apparent we both needed the rest."

"I *never* sleep in the middle of the day!"

She felt his chuckle down to her toes. "You did this time." Did she snore? Help! "I'm going to take it as a compliment you felt comfortable with me."

"In other words it was the proof you needed to realize I don't find you repulsive?"

"Something like that," came the wry comment. "I've already eaten. Have some coffee." He handed her a cup.

"Thank you." She drank half of it before eating a sandwich. In a few minutes she sat back. "That tasted good."

He stood there surfing the channels until he came to another movie. Before she could countenance it, he sat down next to her and pulled her across his lap into his arms.

"This is what I wanted to do earlier."

Andreas moved too fast for her. She could no more resist the hard male mouth clinging to hers than she could stop breathing. Oh—he tasted so good, felt so good. Her body seemed to quicken in acknowledgment that they'd done this before.

Without conscious thought she curled on her side and wrapped her arms around his neck, wanting to get her lips closer to his face. The need to press kisses to each feature took over. She ran a hand into his hair, loving the texture of it.

On a groan he crushed her tighter, then his mouth covered hers again and she thought she'd die of the pleasure he was giving her. "I want you, Gabi. I want to make love to you."

She wanted it, too, more than anything she'd wanted in life, but enjoying a few kisses and sleeping together were two different things. Gabi refused to get in any deeper when she knew she wasn't the only woman in his life. Girlfriend or wife, there *was* someone else. The fact that he still hadn't admitted it revealed the one flaw in him she couldn't overlook.

These last three weeks she'd avoided this situation for the very reason that you couldn't go on kissing each other or it turned into something else. She needed to quit while she could still keep her head. That way she'd have fewer regrets when she got back to the advertising world.

The second he allowed her a breath she eased away from him and stood up. "Much as I'm tempted, I'd rather we didn't cross that line. Remember we're an aunt and uncle to the twins and will be seeing each other on the rare occasion throughout our lives. Many times I've heard you tell potential clients you like keeping things above board and professional. It's my opinion that line of reasoning works well in our particular case."

After his arrival on Milos, Andreas strode through Leon's villa looking for his brother. Estelle told him he was putting the babies down for the night. As he approached the nursery he saw Leon closing the door.

They glanced at each other. "Thanks for coming," he whispered. "Let's go to my room."

"Sorry I couldn't get here any sooner to help with the twins. I had an important meeting." He'd asked Gabi to type up his notes and leave them on his desk before he took off for Milos.

Since the night she'd delivered the coup de grâce, he'd only been functioning on autopilot. Gabi was keeping something from him and he was determined to get it out of her no matter what he had to do.

Leon shut the door behind them. "You're here now. That's all that matters."

Andreas stared at his brother. He'd lost weight and looked tired, but that was to be expected considering he was a new father. The look of anxiety in his eyes was something else again, kindling Andreas's curiosity. "What's this about? I thought you told me Kris was fine after his checkup."

"He is."

"Don't tell me you think they're still missing Gabi?"

"Not as much. After the first few days they both stopped crying for her and accepted me. Now when they see me, they reach for me and don't want anyone else except Gabi when she comes. It's an amazing feeling."

"I can only imagine." Andreas was longing for the same experience himself, but only under the right circumstances. "So what's wrong?"

"Maybe you ought to sit down."

Was it that bad? He remained standing. "Just tell me."

"You won't believe this. Deline called me this afternoon. She's *pregnant*."

The news rocked Andreas back on his heels. In fact it was incredible. He stared at his twin. Leon was now the father of a third child yet to be born.

"The doctor confirmed she's six weeks along. It was the shortest phone call on record. Before she hung up, she said she was still divorcing me, but wanted me to know the baby was due next spring."

"No matter what, congratulations are in order." Andreas gave him a brotherly hug.

Leon looked shell-shocked. "Ironic, isn't it? I've got Thea's children, Deline's carrying mine, yet none of us will be getting together."

He'd left out a heartbroken Gabi who would have had every right to hold on to the twins without telling anyone, but she didn't have a selfish bone in her beautiful body. One thing was evident. Through this experience Leon had learned how much he loved Deline. Andreas could only commiserate with him.

"Don't despair. With time it could all work out the way you want it. As long as I'm here, why don't you fly to Athens and talk to her tonight? I'll do the babysitting duties here until you get back. If you need a couple of days, take it!"

Leon's eyes ignited. "You'd do that?"

His brother was in pain and needed help.

"What do you think?" After today's meeting he didn't have anything of vital importance on for tomorrow. If he went to Gabi's door, she wouldn't let him in. "I'm crazy about my nephews and want to spend some quality time with them."

His brother had difficulty swallowing. "Thanks. It seems like that's all I ever say to you. I haven't been to work in weeks. You've had a double load."

"Don't you remember you've been given maternity leave? As Gabi once said to me, what's sauce for the goose…"

While Leon changed clothes, he shot Andreas a curious glance. "How's she doing as Anna's replacement?"

"Better than even I had imagined."

"Under the circumstances you were wise to break it off with Irena as soon as you did. Everyone in the family knows it now, but I have to tell you it came as a shock to Deline."

Andreas nodded. "Those two managed to grow even closer during the time I was seeing her."

"Deline says Irena is leaving for Italy for a long holiday. Before she does, she wants to take a look at the twins, so don't be surprised if she shows up. Sorry about that if it happens."

"I'm not concerned. If there's any problem with the boys that I don't anticipate, I'll call you."

As soon as Leon left the villa Andreas stretched out on top of his brother's bed and drew the phone from his pocket. He frowned when all he got was Gabi's voice mail. The beep eventually sounded.

"Gabi? Something has come up and Leon needs my help. First thing in the morning I'd like you to reschedule any appointments for the next two days, then I want you to fly to Milos. The helicopter will be standing by. I'll expect you in time to have a late breakfast with the boys."

She would never come for him, but an opportunity to see the twins was something else again.

The apartment in the Simonides office building was more fabulous than any five-star hotel. Every time Gabi stepped out of the shower of the guest suite, she felt as if she were a princess whose days were enchanted because she was allowed to be with Andreas while he worked.

If there was a downside, it came at the end of the day. When Andreas left his office and said he'd see her in the morning, the enchantment left with him. Except for the evening she'd talked to him about not crossing the line, she hadn't been with him in another setting away from the office.

Since she'd come to work for him, the nights had turned out to be the loneliest Gabi had ever known. To stave off the worst of it, she spent time after hours acquainting herself with the files stored on the computer and memorizing the names of his most important clients.

One night last week she'd come across the merger with Paulos Metal Experts. To her astonishment she read that Dimitri had brought several unscrupulous lawsuits against the Simonides Corporation in order to get the judge to intervene.

Andreas had represented his father in court. Every attempt by the opposition was defeated. Photocopies of all the court documents were there. It had been a heated case. She didn't say anything to Andreas, but reading the material gave her a much fuller understanding of the disgusting man Thea had married.

This evening when Andreas had left the office, she could tell he was in a hurry. Naturally she imagined he was planning to spend the night with his girlfriend, a possibility too devastating to contemplate.

With an aching heart she reached for her cell phone to see if there'd been any calls from her parents or Jasmin while she'd been in the shower. To her shock, the only message she'd missed had come from Andreas.

She always loved the opportunity to fly out to Milos so she could hold her precious babies. This time she'd make it a short, drop-in visit and take some pictures of the twins with her cell phone to show her parents. After that she would ask the pilot to fly her to Heraklion for a surprise visit. They'd love to see how much their grandsons had grown.

Since Gabi needed a break to separate herself from Andreas, it was a good plan. In a few more days Kris would be having his surgery. After he'd recovered, she would resign her job with Andreas and go back to Virginia.

That would leave him free to do whatever. Everything would be wrapping up soon and she'd be gone for good.

Twelve hours later Gabi climbed aboard the helicopter atop the office building with her overnight bag. En route to Milos she informed the pilot she would only be there for a brief time. Afterward she wished to be flown to Heraklion.

Armed with her plans, she arrived at the Simonides villa where Andreas stood at the helipad, disturbingly handsome in an unfastened white linen shirt and bathing trunks. She'd been so used to seeing him in a business suit at the office, her heart skipped around, throwing her completely off-kilter.

As he stepped forward to help her out, his penetrating eyes seemed to be all over her, turning her insides to mush. She'd worn a summery print skirt and sleeveless blouse in earth tones on white with white straw sandals. It was an outfit he wouldn't have seen before.

"I'm glad you made it. You smell as delicious as you look this morning."

"Thank you." She hadn't been prepared for a comment like that. Her stomach clenched mercilessly. "It's a new mango shampoo I bought. Your pilot said the same thing. He's going to buy some for his wife."

His white smile was so captivating, her lungs constricted. "I know you can't wait to see the boys. They're in their new swings on the patio. Follow me."

She knew the way as they walked down several flights of steps past flowering gardens to the rectangular swimming pool of iridescent blue.

The Simonides compound was exquisite, surpassing what she'd seen from the air the first time they'd come. Each white villa was terraced with flowers and greenery, one on top of the other all the way down to the sea where the white sand merged with aquamarine waters. She paused on one of the steps to look around.

"Oh, Andreas… I know I say this every time, but this is all so gorgeous, I can't believe it's real." She couldn't believe *he* was real. "With a devoted father like Leon, the children have to be the luckiest little boys on earth."

"The real miracle is that they got their start with you and your family. They're waiting for you."

"I'm dying to see them." She trailed him down one more flight of steps and through an alcove. Out of the corner of her eye she saw the canopied swings propped near each other beneath an overhang of brilliant passion flowers. The seats were moving back and forth to a little nursery-rhyme song.

She ran toward the boys, then slowed down for fear she'd frighten them. They were dressed in identical blue sunsuits. No shoes or socks on because it was too hot.

"They've filled out!"

Andreas chuckled as he undid Kris and handed him to her. "Look who's here."

"Oh, you little sweetheart." She hugged him in her arms, unable to stop kissing his neck and cheeks. While she walked around with him, Andreas extricated Nikos and propped him against his broad shoulder.

"I've missed you," she crooned to him, rocking him gently. Finally she put her head back so she could look at him. "Do you remember me?" He blinked. "I don't think he knows me, Andreas." Her brows furrowed.

"Give him a minute. The sun's so bright. Here. We'll trade." He reached for Kris with one arm and handed Nikos to her with the other.

"How could you possibly be this adorable?" She kissed his tummy. "Do you take cute pills?" She lifted him above her head.

Andreas's happy laughter filled the air. "Kris recognizes your voice. See? He's craning his head to look at you."

"You think?" she cried out joyously. All of a sudden Nikos started getting more excited and made his little baby sounds. "Well, that's more like it." She kissed one cheek, then the other, making him smile each time.

"I'd smile like that if you kissed me that way

all the time," Andreas said in a provocative aside. He was back to being playful.

Gabi ignored the comment, but felt the blush that swept into her cheeks. "I'm not sure this was such a good idea. I don't know how I'm going to tear myself away."

"No one's going anywhere quite yet. Estelle will be out in a minute with their bottles. We'll feed them before she puts them down for their naps."

"Maybe the two of you better do it. I don't want my presence to upset them and undo the progress Leon has made."

She lowered Nikos into his swing so she could take pictures. Now that she had an excuse to capture Andreas at the same time, she took a dozen different shots of him and the children in quick succession.

"It's good for them to see you every few days," he murmured, brushing off her worries. "Their psyches have a greater sense of security knowing you haven't disappeared from their lives."

Gabi squinted at him. "Is that based on scientific fact?"

"No." His lips twitched. "I made it up because I know how much you need to hold them."

I love you, Andreas Simonides.

She found a chair beneath the overhang and put Nikos back on her lap so she could examine him. Andreas pulled up another chair next to her and sat down with Kris. Grasping the children's hands, they started to play pat-a-cake with each other. Gabi broke into laughter. Andreas joined her.

"Maybe we shouldn't interrupt them, Estelle. They're having too much fun."

Gabi heard an unfamiliar female voice and looked over her shoulder. She saw two women, each carrying a baby bottle. The older one was dressed for housework. The younger one was the epitome of the fashionably dressed, breathtaking, black-haired Greek woman, making a beeline for Andreas.

"Irena—" Andreas called to her.

Gabi wished she hadn't seen her. Ever since she'd heard about her from Deline, she'd wondered where she'd been hiding. Now that she'd appeared, Gabi found it was much harder than she'd thought to actually meet her. She hugged Nikos to her body.

Deep inside she wished the vision of this incredibly beautiful female weren't permanently etched in her mind. Her brown eyes looked like velvet. Taking the initiative, Gabi said, "You haven't interrupted anything. I'm Gabi Turner, the boys' aunt."

"How do you do?"

"You've come just in time to help Andreas feed the twins. I can't stay any longer. My parents are expecting me on Crete."

She got up and motioned for Irena to sit down before handing Nikos to her. Andreas's veiled eyes followed her movements. By his enigmatic expression, she had no idea what he was thinking. Estelle handed him the other bottle.

Gabi kissed Nikos before turning to Andreas. "When the pilot flew me here this morning, I hope it's all right that I asked him to wait so he could fly me on to Heraklion."

"Of course," came the low aside.

If Gabi had taken license she shouldn't have, she didn't care. This was one time she needed an escape pod. The helicopter would do nicely. She gave Kris another peck on the cheek.

"See you at the hospital, my little darling." Before she lifted her head, the temptation to cover Andreas's sensuous mouth with her own was overpowering, but she resisted the impulse. "I'll let myself out."

As she hurried to retrace her steps back to the helipad she heard Kris start to cry. A few seconds later Nikos joined in. Their cries brought her pleasure as well as pain. In another minute they'd get over it and enjoy the attention of Andreas and his girlfriend.

Gabi, on the other hand, would never get over it. Her cries were loudest of all, but she would manage to stifle them until after she'd reached Heraklion.

By the time Andreas heard the helicopter and felt the paralyzing pang of watching it swing away with Gabi inside, the twins had settled down enough to finish their bottles.

Irena patted Nikos's back to burp him before putting him in his swing. She glanced at

Andreas. "Forgive me for intruding on you and Gabi, Andreas. I didn't realize you were here this morning."

"You don't owe me any apology. Leon said you might come by to see the babies."

She nodded. "Deline was right. Leon's children are beautiful. What a tragic situation."

Andreas kissed Kris's head. "It's a painful time for everyone concerned including you, Irena. Heaven knows I never meant to hurt you."

"I'm going to be all right."

He had to believe that. "I understand you're leaving for Italy."

"Yes, but I'm glad I came by here first and happened to see you. The change in you since last month has been so dramatic, I don't know you anymore. When I saw you out here with her just now, I felt an energy radiating. It was like a fire burning inside of you. Seeing you with her explains several things I haven't understood and makes me want that kind of love for myself."

He got to his feet. "There's no finer woman than you. You deserve every happiness. How long will you be in Italy?"

"Why do you ask?"

"Because I'm concerned about you."

"Don't be. Your courage to break it off with me has opened my eyes to certain things about myself I haven't wanted to admit or explore. To answer your question, I'll be in Italy for as long as it takes."

Her cryptic remark surprised him. "Irena?"

"Don't say anything more. We already talked everything out at the house. Please don't walk me to the car. You stay with your nephews. *Adio*, Andreas."

"*Adio.*" In a strange way he couldn't decipher, she'd changed, too. Something was going on… Bemused, he watched her until she disappeared, then he looked down at the twins. The time had come to get them out of this heat. He tucked a baby under each arm and carried them back to Leon's villa. Another diaper change and they'd be ready for their naps.

Once the boys were asleep, he found Estelle and told her he was going to do some laps in the pool. The energy Irena had referred to was pouring out of him. He needed to release it with some physical activity or he'd jump out of his skin.

On his tenth lap he heard the sound of a helicopter approaching. His heart knocked against his ribs to think it might be Gabi returning, but that was only wishful thinking. She'd run for her life earlier, just as she'd run from him at Papafragas beach, and again the evening she'd pushed him away at the apartment. He had yet to understand what was holding her back.

The rotors stopped whipping the air. Any member of his family could be arriving from Athens, a constant occurrence during the summer. It was probably one of his sisters with her children.

To his surprise Leon appeared minutes later and plunged in the pool. He swam like a dolphin to reach Andreas. The second he saw Leon's face, he knew the worst without having to be told anything.

"Thanks for watching the boys for me. It was a wasted effort. Deline couldn't get rid of me fast enough. Even with our baby on the way, the divorce is on."

"That's her pain talking right now."

Leon spread his arms and rested his back against the edge of the pool. "Apparently she and Irena have been discussing you and me. Before I left Athens she said, and I quote, 'It looks like your brother doesn't know how to be faithful, either. It must be another twin thing,' unquote."

Andreas frowned. "I don't understand."

"When Deline visited Gabi and the twins in Apollonia, I guess she didn't know you'd already broken off with Irena."

Air got trapped in Andreas's lungs. "You mean—"

"I mean she told Gabi the family was waiting for the announcement that you and Irena would be getting married."

Andreas swore violently and levered himself out of the pool.

"What's wrong, bro?"

"*That's* the reason Gabi's been fighting me." Now it all made sense.

"Ah." He eyed Andreas mournfully. "I wish my problem could be fixed as easily."

So did Andreas. Being twins, they understood each other too well. "I know how much you're hurting over Deline. Don't give up on her."

Leon gave him a mirthless smile. "I couldn't if I wanted to because she *is* the one woman for me. In the meantime the boys are keeping me sane."

"Gabi was here a little while ago. The children started crying when she left. Fortunately they settled down without too much trouble."

"I'm thinking of stealing her away from you," Leon admitted. "I need her help. The twins love Gabi and that's never going to change because she'll always be their aunt. Let's face it. Estelle's way too old for this sort of thing. She's been run ragged the last three weeks. It's not fair to her."

"I couldn't agree more."

"If nothing changes between Deline and me, I'm going to have to hire a permanent nanny. In the meantime I could use Gabi to bridge the gap, especially with Kris's operation coming up soon."

"Then call her!" Andreas cried excitedly. The very prospect had his adrenaline surging.

Leon lifted hopeful eyes to him. "You mean it?"

"Do it now! She can stay in one of the guest villas. Tell her what you just told me and she'll come in a shot. Let her know you're sending the helicopter for her."

His brother darted him a curious glance. "Who'll help you at the office?"

"Christine."

"Gus's private secretary?"

He nodded. "I like her. She's unflappable like Anna."

"Then she's the perfect choice to fill her shoes."

"I'll talk to our big brother. When he understands everything, he'll arrange for her promotion. As soon as you reach Gabi, tell her it's a fait accompli so she won't have any reason to turn you down."

"Who was that on the phone?"

Shaken by the conversation, Gabi hung up and

turned to her mother. They were in the kitchen eating lunch while they looked at the pictures of the babies taken on her cell phone. "It was Leon Simonides. Would you believe his wife is pregnant?"

"You're kidding—"

"No. What's so terribly sad is that she wants the divorce more than ever. He's feeling overwhelmed. His mother has to look after his father, and he's worried because Estelle is too old to keep up the pace. He's asked me to come and help him with the babies until after Kris's operation."

"I don't envy that man the difficult position he's in."

"Neither do I. He's so hurt, Mom." Gabi let out a troubled sigh. "If I'm willing to come, Leon will send a helicopter for me in the morning. All I have to do is say the word and he'll have my personal things moved out of the office apartment to the guest suite on Milos. After the operation he wants me to start helping him interview women for a permanent nanny position."

"That makes sense, but what about your job with Andreas?"

"Leon said not to be concerned. Their other brother's secretary is going to become Andreas's permanent assistant."

He'd already made the arrangements.

Gabi was like a hot potato…so hot Andreas had been willing to let her go without even telling her himself. She couldn't bear it.

Her mother moved around the table and hugged her. "I know you're torn because this means getting closer to the children, but think of it this way. If you decide you want to do this favor for Leon, then staying on Milos will definitely be easier for you."

She looked up at her. "Easier?"

"Oh, darling—I knew you'd fallen in love with Andreas the second he walked in our living room. Knowing he has a girlfriend, this period of time while you've been working for him has to have been very painful."

Gabi buried her face in her hands. "Was I that transparent?"

"Only to your father and me."

After taking a fortifying breath, she lifted her head. "I'll call Leon and tell him yes. With Kris's operation looming, he needs all the support he can get." *And I won't have to face Andreas eight hours out of every day.*

CHAPTER EIGHT

GABI started out her fifth day on Milos with the same routine: baths for the babies followed by a bottle and a morning of playtime out by the pool. As he'd done every morning, Leon had flown to Athens early to put in some work. He always returned by four in the afternoon to take over and give Gabi a break. She'd seen nothing of Andreas, which came as no surprise.

While she was easing Kris into the shallow end of the pool, Estelle appeared. The two of them had developed a friendly rapport. While Gabi did all the carrying and running around, the housekeeper listened for the children when they slept.

"Leonides just phoned. He wants you and the boys to get ready for a boat ride on Andreas's cabin cruiser."

"Did you hear that?" She kissed Kris's cheek.

"Your daddy's on his way home!" Kris's surgery was coming up the day after tomorrow. Since she hadn't been able to stop worrying about it, she welcomed the diversion that put a change in their schedule.

"The maids will pack and carry everything down to the pier. While you get ready, I'll stay with the twins. I've already made up their bottles."

Gabi wrapped Kris in a towel and handed him to Estelle. "I'll be right back."

She darted up the steps to the guest villa to throw on her beach cover-up over her swimsuit. In a bag she stashed a change of outfit, plus a towel and other essentials she might need. When she went back to the pool for the babies, Estelle told her they'd already been taken down to the pier. Leon must have arrived in the helicopter while she'd been packing.

"See you later, then."

Gabi hurried down to the beach and walked along the dock past all the different family ski and jet boats to board the cruiser. She frowned when she couldn't see or hear Leon or the twins.

"Hello? Anyone home?" she called out.

"We're all in the main salon."

She jumped at the sound of Andreas's voice and turned in his direction. The sight of his tall, well-defined body squeezed the air out of her lungs. He stood at the entrance to the companionway in a pair of sweats and nothing else. Beneath his hair more black than night, his silvery eyes swept over her. She might as well have been lit on fire.

"What are *you* doing here? I—I mean I thought you were at work," she stammered.

"At the last minute Leon went to see Deline in the hope that they could really talk. Now that he's found out he's going to be a father again, he's anxious to be with her and know how she's doing. I told him not to worry about his children and flew here as fast as I could."

Gabi was at a loss for words, still trying to recover from seeing him when it was so unexpected.

His lips curved upward, drawing her attention

to his sensuous mouth. "Shall we start again? How are you, Gabi? It seems like months since we last saw each other. I've been all right, but, no matter how efficient Christine is, I must admit I've missed my American secretary who charmed all who came in the office or phoned."

Andreas...

He looked around. "I think it's a beautiful day. What do you think?"

It hurt to breathe. "Is Stavros watching the children?"

"No," he said. "Today we're on our own."

Don't tell me that.

Frightened by the primitive feelings he aroused in her, she darted past him and hurried down the stairs to check on the twins. She found them lying on a quilt he'd placed on the floor of the spacious salon. They were sound asleep on their backs, their arms at their sides with their little hands formed into fists. How would it be?

Andreas had followed her down and stood close enough that she could feel his warmth. "What would it be like to sleep like that without cares or worries? Nothing but sweet dreams until their next meal."

He'd read her thoughts.

"Let's get you up to the helm lounge," he whispered. His breath teased the nape of her neck, sending delicious chills to every part of her body. "I've turned on the intercom down here. If they breathe too hard, we'll hear them."

She didn't need an excuse to put distance between her and Andreas, but she felt self-conscious hurrying up the steps ahead of him. Her sundress only fell to mid-thigh, leaving a good expanse of leg showing.

He led her to the cockpit. "Make yourself comfortable while I untie the ropes. Then we'll be off to some other areas around the island you haven't seen yet."

Gabi sat down on the companion seat next to the captain's chair. Being perched this high with the sun roof open was an experience like no other.

"What do you think?" he asked after taking his seat. His arm and thigh brushed hers, increasing her sensitivity to his touch.

"Like I'm master of all I survey."

A chuckle escaped his lips. "It does feel that way." He started the engine and before long they'd idled out from the bay to head for open water. "When Leon and I were boys, he wanted a huge yacht where he could invite all his friends and sail the seven seas like Ulysses, but I dreamed about owning one of these to go exploring for plunder by myself."

"Naturally." She smiled. Andreas had always blazed his own trails, even if he was an identical twin. "A pirate needs to be able to maneuver in and out of coves, yet be able to outrace his enemies in a big hurry. Now that you've achieved all your dreams, it's going to be our little nephews below who will start dreaming their own dreams."

He cast her a shuttered glance. "You think I've achieved all my dreams?"

She averted her eyes. "It was just a figure of speech."

"For your information, I haven't even begun." He had to be talking about his future with Irena. "What about you?"

They were getting into a painful area. The only dream that truly mattered had been shattered when Deline told her Andreas had gone to Athens to spend time with his girlfriend.

"I've achieved a few little ones."

"For instance?" he prodded.

"I made it into the Penguin club when I was in grade school."

"And that was very important?"

"Yes. You had to be a good ice skater."

"Bravo." She laughed. "What else?"

"In high school I tried to make it on the debate team because I thought those kids were really smart. By my senior year I was chosen."

He turned to look at her. "Was it everything you'd hoped it would be?"

"Anything but. I missed too many classes going to meets, and my egghead partner drove me crazy."

"Male or female?"

"Male."

"I take he didn't grow into one of your past illnesses."

"No. Those came later."

"Have you ever been in love, Gabi? I'm talking about the kind you'd sell your soul for and didn't think was possible. The kind that only comes once?"

He'd just described the condition she was in. A band constricted her breathing. "Yes," she said quietly and got out of the chair. "Excuse me for a moment while I check on the twins."

"We haven't heard a sound from them yet."

"Maybe not, but they might be awake wondering where they are and why their daddy isn't with them. I don't want them to feel lonely."

"They have each other." He looked over his broad shoulder at her. The sun shone down, bronzing his skin. "Take it from me, that's the great thing about twins."

Their gazes fused. "Was it hard at first sharing Leon with Deline?"

An odd silence stretched between them. "Do you know you're the first person who ever asked me that question? You have great perception."

He took his sunglasses from a side pocket and put them on. "To answer your question, *yes*, but it helped that Leon and I do business together.

Sadly it was Deline who suffered the most for having to share him. They'd been quarreling about it the night he took out the yacht with friends and met Thea."

Gabi moaned low in her throat. "After the twins were born, I bought some books to study up on the subject. One of the things I learned was to dress them differently, put them in different classes. Help them to be individuals. But the books also said that there's a bond connecting them like inner radar and has to be allowed for."

"That's true."

"Do you think it will be as hard on Leon when you get married one day?"

"Yes, because he's not used to coming in second with me."

Gabi didn't like playing second fiddle either. Sucking in her breath, she hurried below deck.

After learning the business alongside his father and grandfather, instinct told Andreas when it was the right or wrong time to make a crucial move. Now was not the moment to tell Gabi he was single. She was too worried about Kris and the upcoming surgery.

When the time came, he wanted her full attention in order to gauge her reaction after she learned he was a free man. Until their nephew had recovered and she couldn't use him for a distraction, Andreas would have to hold back, but the operation couldn't come soon enough to suit him.

"Wouldn't you know Kris was awake just lying there looking around making cooing sounds?" She'd returned to the cockpit holding the wide-eyed baby against her shoulder.

At a glance Andreas took in one head of jet-black hair, the other of spun gold. Gabi and child provided a live painting more riveting than the picturesque town in the distance.

"Look how beautiful, little sweetheart!"

Andreas could only echo the sentiment before he had to tear his eyes away and pay attention to steering the cruiser. He'd brought them into an inlet with a sweeping bay.

"Where are we?"

"Adamantas, the social center of Milos. This part of the island has a natural harbor. Everyone prefers this area because it's sheltered from the north winds."

"I'm sure your uncle knows every square inch of this paradise." She spoke to the baby, kissing his cheeks. For a second Andreas closed his eyes, wishing he could feel those lips against his skin, and jaw and lips and mouth. "Between him and your daddy, the day will come when you and Nikos will explore this place on your own. By then your heart will be as strong as your brother's."

Sunlight caught the well of her unshed tears reflecting the same blue as the deep water. The sight of them tugged at his heart. "He's going to be fine, Gabi." For Leon's sake, he *had* to be.

"I know." But the words came out muffled because she'd buried her face in Kris's neck. "He has no idea he'll be going into the hospital tomorrow to be prepped."

"We'll all be with him. I assume you've informed your parents they'll be staying in the guest suite at the office with you."

She lifted her head. "Yes. They're very grateful for everything."

"I've arranged for the helicopter to fly them from Heraklion."

"I know, but they didn't expect that. It's too much."

"The family insists. Our sisters plan to take turns tending Nikos at our parents' home, so there's no worry there."

"I don't think any babies ever had more love, but this has to be so hard on your brother."

Because Leon was his twin, maybe that was the reason Andreas felt the depth of his brother's anguish. "He needs comfort from the wife he has hurt too deeply. It's a tragedy."

"It *is*," she cried softly. "His pain must be exquisite to know she's carrying their child. I'd give anything to help them."

"Gabi," he said huskily, "don't you know you're saving his life right now?"

Her wet eyes swerved to his. "So are you. But who's helping Deline?"

Andreas loved this woman for her compassion. "She has a big supportive family."

"I'm glad for that." He watched her cuddle Kris closer. The pained expression on her face tore him up. In the midst of feeling helpless over her pain, he heard Nikos start to cry.

"I'll get him." He cut the motor and stood up. "When I come back, I'll bring their bottles and carry-cots. Shall I bring the stroller, too? We could go ashore in Adamantas and have a late lunch."

She stared up at him. "Are you hungry?"

He had to be honest. "No."

"Neither am I. Do you mind if we go back? This is a heavenly spot, but when Leon flies here, he'll expect to find his babies waiting for him."

Chills chased down his spine to realize how often he and Gabi were in sync, speaking each other's thoughts. In some ways it was like his connection with Leon, but much stronger.

Before the surgery, both sets of grandparents lingered in Kris's hospital room, hugging and kissing him. Gabi's father was visibly shaken.

She knew he was seeing Thea. With her death so recent, his tears often lurked near the surface.

Leon hadn't let go of his mother. It was very touching. Andreas and their older brother Gus and his wife stood next to their father, who appeared emotional as well. A year ago he'd suffered a heart attack and had to be more aware of his mortality at a vulnerable moment like this.

Gabi found herself studying the impressive, black-haired Simonides family. They were tall people, each one incredibly attractive. Suddenly Andreas looked around and caught her gaze. He gave her a long, unsmiling look that penetrated to her inner core.

She had the feeling he was remembering their first encounter in his office when he was ready to shut the elevator door on her. The newspaper picture and photograph of the twins had changed lives, not only for the families here, but for Deline.

Gabi checked her watch. It was only 6:45 a.m. Kris was the heart surgeon's first patient on the morning docket. She was thankful for that.

They'd all been waiting for this day, each of them doing a mental countdown.

The doctor had told Leon that the newest medical technology had made this a quick procedure. In another hour the surgery would be over. Soon life would return to a new normal, but Gabi couldn't go there yet, not when she knew Andreas wouldn't be in it.

You'd better get used to it, her heart nagged. No more thrilling cruises together with the twins like the one they'd gone on the day before yesterday to Adamantas. As long as she'd been helping Leon through this whole process of getting to know his instant family, Andreas had been a part of it. But those days were numbered and she would never experience such joy again.

She finally broke eye contact with him and hugged her mother, who knew her secret. Gabi needed her strength.

When the door opened, she saw the nurse who'd been working with Leon. She said it was time to take the baby and get the anesthetic administered. "There's a waiting room around the corner. If you'll all move there."

A sob rose in Gabi's throat to see tears trickle down Leon's pale cheeks as he kissed his son one last time. He carried such a load of pain, Gabi marveled at his composure. Andreas was right there to steady his brother as the nurse disappeared out of the room with the baby Gabi had seen born. She felt as if a piece of her heart had been taken away.

Her dad reached for her hand and squeezed it. Slowly everyone filed out to the lounge for the long wait. Time was so relative. When Gabi was with Andreas, laughing and sharing while they played with the twins, an hour was but a moment that flew by unmercifully fast. But this hour was going to take a year to pass, she just knew it.

It didn't surprise her that Andreas was the one who brought in drinks and snacks, waiting on everyone. Before long his brothers-in-law arrived and the men congregated while the mothers started talking. Gus's wife Beril sat by Gabi. She couldn't have been nicer. They spoke quietly about Leon.

"Since becoming a father, he's changed for the

better, Gabi. But taking responsibility has cost him his marriage. I was just talking to Deline yesterday. It's so sad."

Gabi shuddered. "Even though my sister had been drinking, I can promise you she wouldn't have done what she did if she'd known he was married. She wasn't even aware Andreas had a twin brother, but it's far too late to grieve over that now."

Beril wrapped a commiserating arm around her shoulder. Andreas happened to notice the gesture and left the men to come their way, causing Gabi's pulse rate to pick up.

"You look tired," Beril told him.

"Aren't we all, but Leon's the one on the point of exhaustion."

"I haven't had a chance to talk to him yet. Excuse me, Gabi. I'll be back in a minute."

After Beril walked off, Andreas sat down in her place. He smelled wonderful. The creamy sand-colored suit covered his hard-muscled body like a glove. He took her breath. His leg brushed against hers as he turned to her. "Are you all right?" His velvety voice resonated to her insides.

"I will be when the doctor comes in. It's already been an hour and a half. How are you doing?"

"You heard Beril. What can I do for you?"

She glanced at his striking features. Andreas hid his emotions too well. On impulse she said, "I should be asking *you* that question. You've been the one waiting on everyone else."

"Staying busy helps."

As Gabi nodded one of the doctors who'd assisted with the surgery came into the lounge. Like everyone else, she shot to her feet. He looked at Leon.

"Mr. Simonides? Your son's operation was a success, but he's having a little trouble coming out of the anesthetic." Gabi grabbed hold of Andreas's arm without conscious thought. "If you'll follow me. We've got him in the infant ICU."

Leon's anguish was palpable as he eyed Andreas. "Come with me, bro."

Andreas sent Gabi a silent message that he'd

be back and left the room with his twin. Without his support, she hurried over to her parents. Her father hugged her for a long moment.

"I can't believe this is happening, Dad. Leon has already been through so much, and now this… Poor little Kris. He's got to come out of it."

"He will, darling."

When she pulled out of his arms, her mother was there to hug her. "We have to have faith that everything's going to be all right."

While everyone in the room was in agony, Gabi saw something out of the corner of her eye. A dark-haired woman had entered the lounge. It was *Deline*! By then everyone had seen her.

"What's wrong? Where's Leon?" she cried in alarm.

Andreas's mother rushed over to her and explained.

"You mean Kris might not make it?" Deline's voice shook. Her face looked pale.

"None of us is thinking that way."

"But Leon is." Deline's response sounded like a wife who knew her husband better than anyone else. She still loved him, Gabi could feel it. "Where's the infant ICU?"

"Come on, Deline," Gabi answered before anyone else could think. "I'll help you find it."

Together they flew out of the lounge and down the hall to the nurses' station. Gabi spoke up. "This is Mrs. Simonides. She got here late. Her husband is in the infant ICU with Kris who was just operated on. Can she go in?"

"Of course. A baby needs its mother at a time like this." Neither Gabi or Deline bothered to correct the other woman. "Let me get a gown and mask for you."

When Deline was ready the other woman said, "Follow me."

They hurried down another hall and around the corner where they saw Andreas standing outside the door. With the blinds down, you couldn't see inside.

Lines had darkened his arresting face, making him appear older than his thirty-three years. When he saw them coming, his eyes widened in shocked surprise.

The nurse opened the door for Deline who

went right in, then she closed it again and walked away.

In the next instant Andreas gripped Gabi's upper arms. He was so caught up in emotions, he had no idea of his strength. "What's going on?"

Gabi shook her head. "I really don't know. Deline came in the lounge looking for Leon. Your mother told her Kris was in trouble. I thought Deline was going to pass out right there, so I told her to come with me and we'd find them."

Andreas couldn't speak. Instead he put his arms all the way around her and crushed her against him. She understood and didn't misinterpret what was going on while he rocked her.

This whole experience, from the first day Andreas had first found out about the twins, had been so fraught with emotion, he didn't know where else to go with all his feelings. Neither did Gabi, who held on to him, for once not worrying about Irena, who hadn't shared in this life and death situation from the beginning.

"Deline wouldn't have come this morning if she didn't still love Leon," he whispered into her silky gold hair. "She's known about this surgery from the start. To show up today has to mean something, doesn't it?"

Gabi had never heard Andreas sound vulnerable before. It was a revelation. "Yes, I believe it does."

"Oh, Gabi, if I thought—"

"That there might not be a divorce?" she finished what he was trying to say.

"Yes," he cried softly, kissing her forehead and cheeks.

"As my mom said a little while ago, we have to have faith." She buried her face in his neck. "Kris has got to make it, Andreas. Nothing will make sense if he doesn't."

She lost track of time while they held on to each other. This amazing man was actually clinging to her as if his life depended on it. His hands roved over her back. One found its way to her nape. His fingers stroked the curls, sending bursts of delight through her body. Gabi nestled closer against him, loving this feeling of safety and comfort. She'd never known anything like it before.

When another nurse came out of the ICU, Gabi had to force herself away from him, but she wasn't ready for the abrupt separation. It was a good thing there'd been an interruption, otherwise she would have stayed right where she was and Andreas would have figured out what was really going on.

"I'd better get back to the lounge and tell everyone there's been no news about Kris yet." Embarrassed to have revealed her terrible weakness for him, she started down the hall. In one long stride he caught up to her.

"We'll both go. There's no telling how long Leon and Deline will be in there. No matter what's going on with Kris, my brother has the person he wants and needs with him right now. As of this moment, we're both de trop."

Everyone's strained faces turned to them the moment they entered the waiting room. Andreas spoke for them. "We still don't know anything about Kris."

"Is Deline with him?" his mother asked anxiously.

"Yes."

Gabi could hear the questions everyone wanted to voice but didn't dare. "The nurse gave her a gown and mask to put on so she could go in with Leon." She saw glances being exchanged.

Andreas didn't miss them, either. "One thing we all know about Deline. She wouldn't be here at a precarious moment like this to cause Leon pain. Quite the opposite, in fact." He'd championed his sister-in-law. Everything Andreas said or did made Gabi love him that much more.

While he talked with his family, Gabi gravitated to hers, still experiencing the sensation of feeling his arms around her. All that strength was encased in one superb male who worried about his family and still had the stamina to carry the bulk of the load for those depending on him professionally.

She checked her watch for the umpteenth time. Another half hour had passed and still no word about Kris. It wasn't looking good. One glance at her parents' expressions and she knew they were thinking the same thing. The room had grown quiet. Like Gabi, who was fighting not to break down, they were all saying their own silent prayers.

While she was deep in thought she heard Leon's voice. "I have good news, everyone." She looked across the room. His gray eyes shone with a new light. "Kris is awake and breathing on his own. He's going to be all right." His voice broke.

Gabi watched Andreas race toward the entrance to give his brother a bear hug.

"Thank heaven!" She broke down and wept for happiness against her father's shoulder. At that point the whole mood of the room changed to one of jubilation.

"They're going to keep him until tomorrow, then I'll take him home. Deline's going to stay with me and help me." Leon's emotions were spilling out. "Thank you all for being here. I couldn't have gotten through this without you."

After hugging everyone, he hurried out of the

room taking Andreas with him. No doubt he needed to talk to his twin privately.

Gabi's heart failed as she watched him disappear. Dying inside, she turned to her mother. "Mom?" she whispered. "Do you mind if we go back to the apartment and pack? I'd like to fly to Heraklion today, but let's go by plane. Even though Andreas has put the helicopter at our disposal, I don't want to take advantage now that Leon doesn't need me to help with the babies."

"I think that's a very wise idea." Her mother understood everything. "Let's go."

Once outside the hospital, they took a taxi back to the Simonides office building. Gabi put in the code so they could ride the private elevator to her floor. Relief that Kris was going to be all right took away all their anxiety in that regard, but Gabi was in too much pain over leaving Andreas to talk.

A clean break.

That was what she'd done with the twins a month ago. Now it was time for one more. She turned off her phone.

Her parents traveled a great deal so it didn't take them long to gather up their things and head for the airport in a taxi. While at the Athens airport waiting for their flight, she made the reservation for her trip to Washington, D.C., leaving the next day.

By late afternoon they reached the consulate. After a quick meal, Gabi showered and changed out of her suit into straw-colored linen pants and a mocha blouse in a silky fabric. With too much nervous energy to sit still, she got started on some serious packing. When she'd come here—five months ago now—she'd brought a lot of clothes. Enough to fill two suitcases and an overnight bag.

She'd left home in March and would be arriving in the August heat. An oppressive heat without the relief of a shimmering blue sea wherever you turned—without a pair of black-fringed gray eyes wandering over you like the sun's reflection off the water.

Gabi couldn't breathe for thinking about so many moments with Andreas preserved in her memory. Earlier today her body had memorized the feel of his while they'd held on to each other outside the ICU. She'd known it would be for the last time. That was why she hadn't been able to let go.

"Gabi?" Her father walked in her room. "I guess you didn't hear me. There's a man in the foyer wishing to speak to you. He says his name is Stavros."

She felt a quickening in her body. What kind of errand had Andreas sent him on? Her heart pounded so hard she got light-headed.

"What's wrong, honey? You paled just now. Who is he?"

"He crews for Andreas. I like him very much."

"Then you'd better not keep him waiting."

"You're right."

The urge to fly down the stairs was tempered by her fear that Stavros would know how excited she was. But that was silly because he was observant enough to know she was so hopelessly in love with Andreas, it hurt. He'd watched her in unguarded moments around his boss. She doubted anything got past him, either.

"It's nice to see you again, Stavros."

He smiled. "You, too. I brought the cabin cruiser over from Milos for Kyrie Simonides. A family gathering kept him in Athens longer than expected. His helicopter should be landing any minute now. To save time, he asked me to escort you on board and he'll join you for dinner to say goodbye."

That was the longest speech she'd ever heard him give, but the answer was still "no." No more. She couldn't take seeing him again.

"That sounds lovely. Please tell him thank you, but I'm flying to the States in the morning and have too much to do."

"I'll tell him." He started to leave, then stopped. "I shouldn't say this because it will spoil his surprise, but he's got Nikos with him."

Nikos—

Stunned by what he'd just told her, she was slow on the uptake. "Wait—" she cried because the taxi he'd taken here was about to leave. "I'll come. Give me a minute to grab my purse."

She dashed upstairs for it. When she returned,

her parents were talking to Stavros. "We heard," her mom said. "Give Nikos a hug for us."

Five minutes later the taxi dropped them off at the pier where she could see the cabin cruiser moored. As she stepped on deck Andreas came out holding Nikos against his shoulder.

She moaned inwardly because they looked perfect together, but it was all wrong. In an ideal world, Nikos should be Andreas's son... and *hers*.

He flashed her one of his enticing smiles. "We're glad you came, aren't we, little guy?" Andreas turned the baby so he could see her. Nikos's eyes lit up. He acted so happy to see Gabi, she let out a joyous laugh and pulled him into her arms.

"How's my big boy?" After smothering him with kisses, she carried him to the rear cockpit. Over his black curls she studied Andreas, who was standing there with his powerful legs slightly apart, looking impossibly handsome in a black crew neck and jeans. "This was a totally unexpected surprise. Thank you." Her voice caught.

"I knew you had to be missing him." His eyes narrowed on her upturned features. "It appears this was a day of surprises on both our parts, starting with your flight to Heraklion."

All of a sudden Gabi started to feel uncomfortable.

"I won't bother to ask why you didn't use the helicopter or why you didn't stay at the apartment long enough for me to take you and your parents out to dinner."

She hugged Nikos tighter. "We would have enjoyed that, but Leon needed you and you had your whole family to deal with."

"And?" he prodded.

"I didn't say anything else."

"Yes, you did," he came back more aggressively. She moved Nikos to her other shoulder and gave him kisses. "You were going to add Irena's name to the list."

Gathering up her courage, she asked, "What kept her from being at the hospital with you?"

"I didn't invite her."

"Andreas—" She stared at him, baffled. "That doesn't sound like you."

One eyebrow lifted. "An interesting observation. It connotes you're somewhat of an expert on my psyche. I like that," he drawled.

Gabi clung to the baby, growing more nervous by the second. "I shouldn't have said anything."

"You can say anything you like to me."

Exasperated, she cried, "That's what I mean—you're normally so warm and kind about everyone. Did you and Irena quarrel? Otherwise I can't imagine her not being with you this morning w-when—"

"It was a life and death situation?" he finished for her.

"Something like that, yes." Getting agitated, she walked Nikos over to the windows looking out on the harbor. "I'm sure she's been upset since the moment she heard about this whole situation with the twins. But she doesn't have to worry now. The children are settled with their father and I'm leaving tomorrow so—"

"Gabi—" he broke in. "Before you say another word, there's something you need to know."

She struggled for breath. "What?"

"A week ago I learned from Leon that Deline had come to visit you and the twins in Apollonia. I understand she mentioned I'd gone to Athens to see my girlfriend Irena Liapis, the woman who was going to become my wife. Did I repeat that back to you correctly?"

Her body shuddered. "Yes."

He stared her down. "It's too bad Deline wasn't apprised of all the facts at the time."

"What facts?" she whispered.

"That I'd already broken it off with Irena. It's true that she used to be my girlfriend."

Used to be? Gabi's heart jumped. "But Deline said your family was expecting you to marry her."

"Up until you came to my office, that was my intention. Needless to say, my entire world got knocked off its foundation the moment I saw that photo of the twins. In order to deal with the ramifications of your unexpected visit, I was forced to put any plans I had on hold."

"Andreas..."

"As it turned out, it was a good thing. The time away from her made me realize that if I'd loved her the way a man should love a woman, we would have been married months earlier."

"How can you say that?" she cried. "I saw the look on her face when she came to the villa and saw us together with the children."

"What you saw was surprise that we were both there instead of Leon. She's very close to Deline and came by to see the famous Simonides twins before leaving for Italy on vacation."

By now Andreas had made himself comfortable on the leather bench with his arms outstretched and his hard-muscled legs extended in front of him. "Now that Kris is out of the woods, I thought we could relax over dinner and talk."

"There's nothing to discuss." She sank down opposite him, still holding Nikos, who seemed to be content for the moment.

"You've made up your mind to leave, then?"

Her brows met in a frown. "You *know* I have."

"Would you mind putting it off one more day?"

Yes, she'd mind. It would kill her to be around

him any longer. "I can't. After I got back with my parents, I phoned my boss at the advertising agency. He's meeting me for lunch the day after tomorrow to discuss my new promotion."

"I'm sorry to hear you're flying out that soon," he murmured. "Nikos and I will be disappointed. We were hoping to enjoy your company for another day."

Another day is all he wants, Gabi. Not a lifetime.

She kissed the top of the baby's head. "Why isn't he with your sisters?"

"They've already taken turns watching him. Now it's my turn to be responsible. If all goes well, Leon's bringing Kris home from the hospital tomorrow. He and Deline will need time alone with him, so I won't return Nikos until the day after tomorrow and could use your help. Our little nephew loves the sea. What better way to tend him than to cruise around parts of the island tomorrow you haven't seen?"

He sat forward with his hands clasped between his strong legs, staring at her in that disturbing way that made her palms ache. "If you hadn't turned off your phone, I wouldn't have had to come all this distance to ask for your cooperation."

Her cheeks went hot.

"I'd like to think we can return him to Leon in good shape. Of course if another day away from Virginia jeopardizes your chances of being promoted, then I'll call for a taxi to drive you to the consulate. The decision is up to you."

Another twenty-four hours with Andreas… Unlike Leon with Thea, Andreas hadn't proposed they spend a night of passion together and then go their separate ways. Otherwise he wouldn't have brought the baby with him.

To Gabi's shame, *she* was the only person who couldn't be trusted in this situation. Andreas had asked her to help him take care of Nikos as a favor to his brother, nothing more. Tears stung her eyelids. Gabi loved Andreas desperately, but he didn't love her.

She nestled Nikos closer. What this all added up to was that Andreas had a kind streak, stronger than most people's. He'd known she would have adopted the children if things hadn't worked out. This last twenty-four hours had been offered as a gift before he let her go back to where she came from.

Clearing her throat, she said, "I didn't bring anything with me except my purse."

"That's not a problem," came his deep voice. "Your cabin has cosmetics. There's a robe and extra swimsuits for guests. You really won't need anything else."

She was dressed in her linen pants and blouse. Since they weren't going to do anything but be on the cruiser, she supposed he was right and could feel herself weakening. She hated her weakness.

"I'll have to phone my parents and my old boss." She also needed to change her plane reservation.

Andreas reached for the baby. "While you do that, I'll feed this little guy. It's after seven. He's starting to look around for his bottle."

She waited until he'd gone below deck before phoning her family. After three rings her mother answered. Gabi explained she was still with

Andreas, but her mom sounded upset when she told her about his plans.

"Darling? You're a grown woman capable of making your own decisions, but for what it's worth, I don't think this is a good idea. You have to look after yourself now. You're going back home with a broken heart. Do you really think it's wise to prolong the inevitable?"

"No."

"Of course you want extra time with Nikos, but Andreas doesn't need you to help him tend the baby."

"I know."

"I can tell I've said too much. Forgive me. All I want is your happiness, and there hasn't been a lot of that since you flew to Greece after Thea became so ill."

She gripped the phone tighter. "You haven't said anything I haven't been telling myself since I first met him. Thanks for being my mom." Her voice caught. "When I hang up, I'll give Nikos a kiss and come home. See you in a little while."

CHAPTER NINE

A BRUSH through her curls and a fresh coat of lipstick helped Gabi pretend she was in control before she went down the companionway to say a final goodbye. Midway to her destination she could hear the sounds of bossa nova music playing quietly in the background.

Before she stepped onto the floor of the main salon, a slight gasp escaped her throat to see an elegantly decorated table with candles and fresh pink roses. Their sweet scent filled the room.

As she looked around her gaze caught sight of Andreas coming out of the galley with two plates of food. Her heart thumped loud enough for him to hear. "Where's Nikos?"

Andreas put the plates on the table. "Good evening, Gabriella Turner. I'm glad you could make it. Nikos fell asleep after his bottle waiting for you. I put him in my stateroom, but left the door open in case he wakes up for some reason."

The next thing she knew he held out a chair for her. "Please sit down and we'll take advantage of this wonderful Brazilian meal Stavros has prepared for us. It's a specialty of his due to his part-Brazilian nationality." She didn't know that. "He's really outdone himself tonight."

No one in the world had charm like Andreas. Now more than ever she needed to keep her wits about her. The romantic ambience was too much. "I agree everything's lovely, but—"

"No buts or you'll hurt his feelings. He's grown very fond of you and the twins. So have I. Since you first came to my office, all you've done is sacrifice for me and Leon, not to mention our entire family. It's time you were waited on for a change. With this meal, please accept the gratitude of the Simonides clan."

Gratitude?

Suffering another heartsick pang, she sat down across from him. When the meal was over she would thank him and Stavros. Following that, she would leave the cruiser without tiptoeing in the other room to give Nikos one last kiss.

The fabulous *churrasco*, a beef barbecue served on skewers, made a wonderful change from the Greek food she'd enjoyed for the last four months, yet she had to force herself to eat. To her chagrin she'd lost her appetite knowing she wouldn't be seeing Andreas again. His keen eyes couldn't help but notice.

He lifted his wineglass and took a sip, eyeing her over the rim. The candlelight flickered in his eyes, bringing out the flecks of silver that made them so beautiful. "Who would have dreamed when you swept into my office, things would turn out the way they have?"

She wiped the corner of her mouth with a napkin. "We can only hope Deline's decision to go back to Leon is permanent."

Andreas breathed in sharply. "He's a changed man. By the time baby three comes along, he ought to be an expert in fatherhood. That ought to be good for something."

Gabi heard the concern in his voice and wanted to comfort him. "Since Thea isn't alive, I'd like to think it will be easier for Deline to love the babies for themselves, especially after she's had their baby."

"Let's hold that thought," he said in a purring voice. "More wine?"

She shook her head. "I haven't even finished what I have." Her gaze happened to flick to the half-full glass. She noticed the liquid moving. It suddenly dawned on her she could hear the motor of the cruiser. They were skimming the placid water at full speed!

Only now and then did she feel the vibration from another boat's wake. Gabi had been so deep in thought about Deline and Leon, she hadn't noticed.

"We've left the port—" she cried in panic.

He nodded, not acting in the least perturbed. "Why are you so surprised?"

Her hand went to her throat in a nervous gesture. "Because I'd decided to go home after dinner. You don't need me to help take care of Nikos. I realize you only did this to let me have a little more time with our nephew, but the gesture wasn't necessary."

Though he didn't move, if she weren't mistaken his eyes darkened with some unnamed emotion. "We're at least a third of the way to Milos, but if you want Stavros to turn back, I'll tell him."

"No—" She rubbed her temples where she could feel the beginnings of a tension headache coming on. "Since we're that far out to sea, I'm not going to ask you to change your plans now." She was such a little fool.

"You look pale. What's wrong?"

"Probably nothing a walk up on deck in the night air won't cure. Please excuse me. The dinner was outstanding. I'll be sure to let Stavros know."

She pushed herself away from the table and rushed up the stairs. When she reached the rear cockpit, she could still hear the Latin music. Her blood throbbed with the beat. The urge to dance right into Andreas's arms was becoming a violent need.

Out here on the water there was a stark beauty to the seascape. It provided another haunting memory to take home with her.

"Feeling better?"

She hadn't realized he'd come up on deck. Andreas moved with the quiet stealth of a gorgeous black leopard. Swallowing hard, she said, "Much, thank you."

"I checked on Nikos. He's in a deep sleep."

"That's good." He stood too close to her. She moved to the leather bench and sat down to look out of the windows.

"Aside from missing your parents and the twins, are you looking forward to going home to the States?"

"Yes," she lied. "I love the work I do."

"They'll be lucky to get you back. If you ever need a reference, I'll vouch for you in the most glowing terms."

"Thank you." Unable to sit still, she stood up again. "If you'll excuse me, I'm going to go to bed."

"It's not that late. There's going to be a moon like the kind you don't see very often."

"I'm sure that's true." She clasped her hands together. "But I'm afraid I won't be able to stay awake. It's been a long day, and the wine has made me sleepy."

He rubbed the pad of his thumb along his lower lip. "You only drank half a glass."

Nothing escaped him. "It doesn't take much for me. Goodnight." She made it as far as the entry when he called her name. She swung around and looked back at him. His hooded gaze disguised any emotions he was feeling. "Yes?"

"I'm curious about something. How did working for me compare to the work you do for your boss?"

Gabi couldn't understand why he'd asked her that. "They're both very challenging in their own ways." If she stayed on deck any longer, he'd break her down and get the truth out of her. Then she'd really want to sink in a hole and hide from him. "Where will we be docking in the morning?"

"Why?" he demanded with an edge to his tone. "Are you hoping it will be at the villa so you can fly back to Heraklion in my helicopter?"

"Only if it won't put you out."

"How could it do that?"

His mood had changed. She'd angered him when it was the last thing she'd wanted to do. "I think you're tired, too. The strain of Kris's surgery has caught up with both of us. Get a good sleep, Andreas. I'll see you in the morning."

Without waiting for a response, she went down to her cabin. Once she'd checked on the baby to make sure he was still sleeping comfortably, she showered and went to bed using the guest robe hanging on the bathroom door. Surprisingly, she slept until Nikos woke her up at six wanting to be fed.

After dressing in the same outfit she'd worn last evening, she took off his diaper and bathed him. He loved the water and wanted to play. Finally she dressed him and put him in his carry-cot. On the way to the cockpit, she got his bottle out of the fridge in the galley and carried him up on deck to feed him.

To her surprise the cruiser was moored at a pier along a stretch of beach she'd never seen before. Because it was dawn, the layers of hills in the light above the sand took on lavender to purple hues with each receding line.

At the top of the first hill a small, white cycladic church was silhouetted against the sky. The sheer beauty of it stood out and drew her gaze. She realized she was looking at a sight quite out of this world. A glimpse of Olympus?

"This is my favorite spot on Milos in the early morning," came the familiar male voice she loved. "Before you went home I wanted you to see it at first light."

She cast him a sideward glance. "I can see why. It would be impossible to describe this to anyone and do it justice. This is something you have to experience for yourself."

Andreas lounged against the entry, focusing his gaze on the church. "I was a boy when my parents first brought me here. I thought it had to be the home of the gods."

"Would you believe I thought the same thing when I came up here just now?"

His eyes found hers. They seemed to be asking something of her. "How would you like to go up there? It's a bit of a climb, but not difficult and won't take long. Stavros will watch Nikos for us."

All the warning bells were going off telling Gabi not to go, but she sensed this was too important to Andreas to turn him down. He wanted her to see a place that had deep meaning for him. She knew he didn't show this private side of him to very many people.

She felt honored. Even if she could never have this man's love, she had garnered his respect and that was something to treasure. "I'd like that."

Andreas pulled out his cell phone and told Stavros they were going ashore for a little while. Within seconds the older man arrived at the cockpit with a smile.

"I'll take good care of the little one."

Gabi thanked him for the lovely dinner and his willingness to tend Nikos. "We won't be long," she assured him.

"Shall we go?" Andreas led the way off the boat and along the pier. This morning he was wearing white pants and a sport shirt in a dusky blue silk. She couldn't take her eyes off him.

As he ambled up the path she could imagine

him as a boy. She ached to think she'd only known him a short time. All those years when she'd missed the in-between part were gone. She would never know the rest of the years yet to come…

A debilitating stab of pain took the wind out of her. She had to stop halfway up the path in order to gather her strength so she could keep moving. Finally they reached the top. From this vantage point she had an incredible view of the Aegean a thousand feet below.

Andreas turned to her with those penetrating eyes. "What do you think?"

"You didn't really need to ask me that."

A smile broke out on his face so beautiful, she had trouble breathing. "Years ago couples wound their way up from the village on the other side to be married here, but the tradition dwindled out because the guests weren't up to it."

She laughed, still out of breath herself. "Nowadays it would have to be the rare couple who…" The rest of the sentence didn't come out. Why did he mention that subject? Bringing Gabi here was too cruel. She knew he hadn't meant to be, but she couldn't take anymore.

"I—I think we'd better get back to Nikos."

"We just got here." His unflappable manner was starting to unnerve her. He moved closer. "I want to take you inside. The priest came early and opened it especially for us. He's anxious to meet you."

Gabi blinked. "I don't understand."

"Maybe this will help." In the next breath he pulled her into his arms and lowered his compelling mouth to hers in a kiss of such intense desire, he set off a conflagration inside her. It went on and on, deeper and longer and so thrilling, her legs shook.

"With every breath in my body, I love you, Gabi Turner. I want you for my wife and have asked the priest to marry us. Everything's been arranged."

"But I thought—"

"You think too much. I've wanted this since the moment you came into my life."

His electrifying tone and the fire in his eyes caused her to tremble. She could hear him talking, but she couldn't believe any of this was really happening.

"Little did I know that the minute Kris survived his operation, you would try to get away from me. You do love me, don't you? Say it—I've been dying for you to admit it."

"I would have said it weeks ago," she cried, throwing her arms around his neck so she could cover his face with kisses. "I'm in love with you, darling. I don't know if you're in my dream, or I'm in yours, but it doesn't matter because I've needed this forever."

His mouth sought hers again and they clung in a rapture that swept her away. He cupped her face in his hands. "Tell me I'm the man you were talking about," he demanded almost savagely. "Admit it," he cried.

"You *know* you are," she said with her heart in her eyes reflecting the lavender light. "I love you so desperately you can't imagine, Andreas." Now that he'd kissed her again, she was addicted to his mouth, seeking it over and over in an explosion of need, yet the terrible hunger they had for each other kept on growing.

At last he drew in a harsh breath. "There's no way I would ever let you go. I'm in love with you, Gabi. The kind I didn't think would ever happen to me. The way I feel about you, we have to get married *now*."

Gabi needed no urging. He grasped her hand and led her inside the small, seventeenth-century church where he'd come as a boy. The robed priest was waiting for them. She felt as if she were floating in a dream, but it seemed real enough by the time he'd pronounced them husband and wife.

Andreas turned to her with a look of eager, tremulous joy. "Let's go, Mrs. Simonides."

Like happy children let out of school, they ran down the path to the waiting cruiser far below. When they reached the bottom, Andreas swept her in his arms. "I've been wanting to do this for weeks."

"Congratulations on your marriage," Stavros called out while her husband was kissing her senseless. "Don't worry about Nikos. He's up in the cockpit with me learning the ropes."

* * *

"Have I worn you out yet?" Andreas whispered against her throat. It was already early evening. Only temporarily sated, they were wrapped together on their sides, still unwilling to let each other go, even to sit up.

She stared into his adoring eyes. "I'm ashamed to admit that will never happen. I can't remember when I wasn't in love with you."

"The evening you stood at the elevator in my office fighting for our nephews' lives, I found out what the meaning of real love was all about. It hit me so hard and fast, I'll never be the same."

Her eyes misted over. "I knew how deeply I loved you when I saw you interact with the twins. The kind of caring you showed them and your brother told me this was a man above the rest and the woman lucky enough to win his love would be the happiest woman alive."

She caressed the side of his firm jaw. "I'm that woman, Andreas. You make me so happy, I'm frightened."

His expression sobered. "So am I. Joy really

does exist for some. We have to guard it with our lives, *agape mou*."

She nodded, pressing her mouth to his, loving the taste and feel of him. "It's so sad that Thea never found it."

He pulled her on top of him. "My poor brother came too close to losing it. I swear I'll love you till the day I die."

The second his hungry mouth closed over hers, Gabi let out an ecstatic sigh, needing her husband's possession. How had she lived this many years without him? Time didn't exist as they gave each other pleasure almost beyond bearing.

"Uh-oh," she whispered into his hair some time later. "I think I heard a little cherub who's been ignored too long."

Andreas bit her earlobe playfully. "I'll get him."

In half a minute he'd brought the baby to bed with them. He lay him on top of his chest, a position Nikos didn't like as well as on his back.

"Oh, Andreas…isn't he the most adorable child you ever saw?"

"Thea and Leon did good work, didn't they?"

"Yes," she admitted with a gentle laugh.

His smoldering gaze found hers. "I can do good work, too."

Emotion made her voice husky. "I already know that."

"Will you be disappointed if our first baby isn't a twin? I'm not unaware you'd planned to adopt these two."

"That was the original plan." She kissed Andreas's shoulder. "But when I saw Leon with them in Apollonia, the ache for them passed because another ache had taken over. I discovered I wanted my own babies with you."

"Gabi..."

Somehow they got lost in another kiss, but Nikos didn't like being caught between them and made his discomfort known.

"It's okay, little guy." Andreas lifted him in the air and got to his feet. "Estelle's waiting to take care of you tonight." He put him in his carry-cot and got dressed.

Gabi sat up in the bed, taking the sheet with her. "She is?"

"Since we're on our honeymoon, she insists. When we get back in the morning, we'll fly to Athens with Nikos and tell everyone our news, then we'll head straight to Crete. In the meantime, I want you to stay in that bed and wait for me. I won't be long."

"You'd better not be. I already miss you."

He shot her a sizzling glance. "You don't know the half of it, but you're going to find out."

A thrill ran through her body. She ached with love for him. The moment he disappeared with her precious Nikos, she got out of bed and threw on her robe. Her purse was in her cabin. She padded out of the stateroom to get her phone and call her parents, who were delighted with the happy news.

"Well, we'll see you tomorrow, then, darling," her dad said, clearing his throat. "Tell Andreas welcome to the family."

She already had...in ways that would make her blush over the years.

"I will. See you tomorrow. Love you."

No sooner had she hung up than she could hear Andreas calling to her. "I'm in my cabin!"

He came to the door out of breath, his eyes alive. "What are you doing in here?"

"I was just letting Mom and Dad know our news. They're thrilled out of their minds."

"So am I," he murmured, taking her down on the bed with him. "I told Stavros to head for Papafragas beach. If no one's around, I want to make love to you there. It's one of my many fantasies since you blew into my life."

She kissed his eyes and nose. "That's twice you've used that expression."

"Because you're like a fragrant breeze that blows across the island, filling me with wants and needs beyond my ability to express."

"I love you so much I'm in pain, Andreas."

"So am I, and plan to do something about it right now. We can either swim in like we did before, or we can take the shortcut down the steps to the sand from the other side."

She let out a squeal. "There's a shortcut?"

He burst into deep laughter, the kind that rumbled out of him. "So I *have* worn you out."

"Never. But right now I'd rather reserve all my energy for loving you. How long before we get there?"

Andreas undid the sash on her robe. "Long enough, my love."

CHAPTER TEN

AFTER making love over and over again, they lay entwined on the sand until it gave up all its heat. By the middle of the night, Andreas had to throw a light blanket over them.

"Look at those stars, darling. With the walls on either side of us, it's like viewing the heavens through a telescope."

"I *am* looking," he answered her. "They're in your eyes." He couldn't believe he was actually holding his wife, his lover, his best friend. His *life*.

She gave him that special smile he felt wrap right around his heart. He needed to love her all over again. "When we bring our children here one day, we can never tell them…well, you know."

Gabi could be bold one minute, shy the next. Always the giver. There was so much to learn about her. Thank heaven this was only the beginning.

"You mean how we consecrated this spot for our own?" he whispered against her throat.

"Yes."

"I came close to ravishing you on this sand before."

"I came even closer to letting you," she confessed. "You'll never know how much I wanted you that night."

He expelled a sigh. "I wasn't sure of you then. Irena told me that when she saw us together, she felt this energy radiating from us like a fire had been lit."

"Andreas—" She clasped him tighter. "Here I am with you—all of you—I have you totally to myself—and I still want more. Maybe there's something wrong with me to love you this much."

He kissed her trembling lower lip. "If there is, I don't ever want you to get well."

"This night is enchanted. I wish we could hold back the morning. It's going to be here before we know it."

"The morning will always have its enchantment, Gabi. That's because, no matter where we are, we'll always wake up to each other."

"Promise me," she cried urgently.

His adorable wife loved him as much as he loved her. Before the joy of it gave him a heart attack, he proceeded to convince her that this was only the beginning.

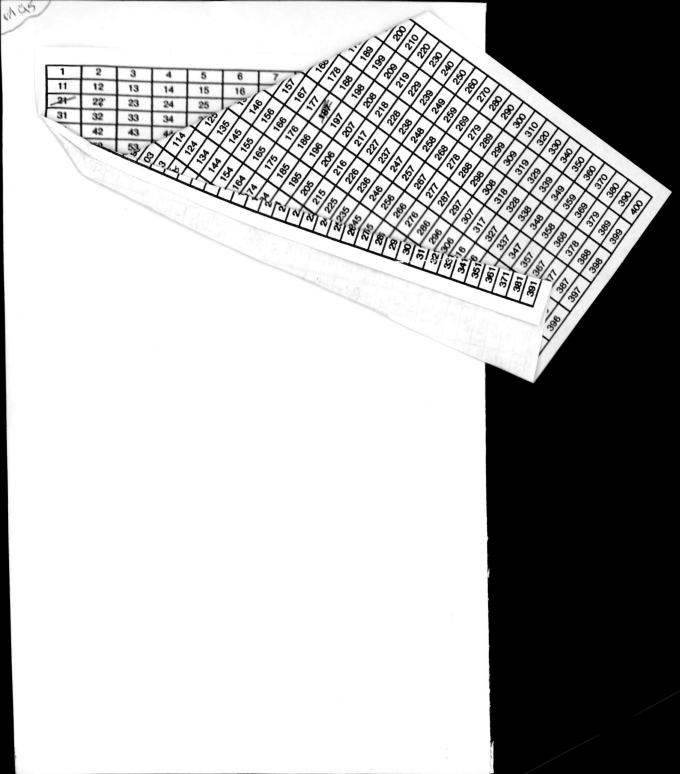